THE ARMOR GIVER

This is a book that I highly recommend. It's a combination of the modern-day "The Pilgrim's Progress" and "The Chronicles of Narnia" book, brought to life with vivid, magical scenery and deeply relatable characters.

As a grandparent, I found the story of the Family of Seven particularly touching and meaningful.

Each member's unique struggles resonated with me, and I believe both kids and adults will see a bit of themselves in these characters.

The adventure of escaping darkness and confronting a Wizard isn't just thrilling; it beautifully imparts the importance of understanding and memorizing God's words.

This book gave me a wonderful way to share with my grandchildren the significance of hiding God's words in their hearts, and the lessons of love, perseverance, and the promise of reunion.

The story is so vivid, it felt like a movie playing in my mind. I wholeheartedly recommend this enchanting and instructive book to parents, grandparents, and children.

It's a perfect blend of entertainment and life lessons, teaching young readers about love, hope and faith.

—**Nony Lukito-Lim,** Current Business owner of *Financial Services & Insurance Agency, California*, Author of *teenage books and short stories in Indonesia*

***

Engaging and Inspirational: A Must-Read Adventure

The Armor Giver: Alwind's Tale is a captivating story, poised to become a classic. This beautifully written book skillfully blends adventure with profound lessons, making it an approachable yet impactful read, much like "Pilgrim's Progress" and the "Wingfeather Saga" series.

Here's a world where the battle between good and evil is palpable, and the resolve to never give up is paramount. The story revolves around a group of inspiring children whose bravery and loyalty will resonate with readers of all ages. Sean, the eldest, is driven by his quest to understand the Armor Giver and protect his family. Kayleigh, with her love for nature and willingness to help, balances her nurturing spirit with a sense of duty. Hugh's kindness and determination lead him down dangerous paths, while Fiona's songs and dances bring hope and joy to her family. Young Liam, the embodiment of hope, rounds out this courageous group.

Each character in this tale is well-crafted, adding depth to the narrative and providing readers with relatable and inspiring heroes. The adventures they embark on are filled with thrilling moments and teach valuable lessons about courage, resilience, and the power of hope.

The Armor Giver: Alwind's Tale is an exceptional book that should be on everyone's reading list. Whether you're a fan of adventurous tales, moral conflicts, or stories of unwavering perseverance, this book will not disappoint. It's a must-read for anyone seeking a story that is both entertaining and enriching.

Prepare to be hooked from the first page to the last – *The Armor Giver* is a journey you won't want to miss!

—Ana Leyva, Founder of *@leluusa*, Startup Advisor at *Pear VC*, Mother of 3

***

Refreshing and riveting story of a family's journey! The parents are raising their children in the time-honored virtues and values. They are the beacon of lights to the children's pathway in life. The children are unique in numerous ways, but the parents' guiding principles are consistent, loving, and profoundly wise. The children's strengths and weaknesses are highlighted in every situation they encounter, but they would always go back to what they learned and are learning from their parents. These parenting approaches and behaviors are worth emulating.

I highly recommend this book! Everyone can glean lessons which are applicable and noteworthy. It communicates and conveys how to be a family during joyful, as well as daunting and dreadful situations. Once one starts, it is difficult to stop reading, because the story captivates your heart!

—Frances Leonor, PhD, Past School Principal/School Administrator, *Highlands Christian Schools*, Adjunct Professor, *Concordia, University Irvine*, Educational Consultant

***

Laura Quinn's *The Armor Giver: Alwind's Tale,* is an engaging story that follows a young family on a journey as they encounter light and darkness, good and evil. From the very first pages, I was drawn into their trek as the family encounters various forms of darkness, from subtle temptations to overt evil. Yet, in these challenges, the characters also experience the power of light, hope, and redemption. Quinn leads readers through themes of faith, trust, and the importance of spiritual armor in the face of adversity. It is a wonderful story for children to read alone, or even better, as a family read aloud. Readers are sure to enjoy and be engrossed in Quinn's tale of adventure and allegory, relating to the characters in their struggles and, ultimately, in their triumphs. I enthusiastically recommend this book to children and families.

—Jill Halverson, International Project Director, latm.info

THE ARMOR GIVER

ALWIND'S TALE

LAURA QUINN

Published by KHARIS PUBLISHING, an imprint of KHARIS MEDIA LLC.

Copyright © 2025 Laura Quinn
ISBN-13: 978-1-63746-277-5
ISBN-10: 1-63746-277-8
Library of Congress Control Number: 2024950270

Illustrator: MJ Quinn

All rights reserved. This book or parts thereof may not be reproduced in any form, stored in a retrieval system, or transmitted in any form by any means - electronic, mechanical, photocopy, recording, or otherwise - without prior written permission of the publisher, except as provided by United States of America copyright law.

All KHARIS PUBLISHING products are available at special quantity discounts for bulk purchase for sales promotions, premiums, fund-raising, and educational needs. For details, contact:
Kharis Media LLC
Tel: 1-630-909-3405
support@kharispublishing.com
www.kharispublishing.com

KHARIS PUBLISHING

For my Husband and children. In this, you will see how much each of you have inspired me. In each of us we hold strengths and weaknesses but with love at the center of us we have overcome and journeyed many adventures – always together. Thank you.

And to the Armor Giver – my hope is that this book shows just how loving and caring you truly are and perhaps a few will find your narrow path or find a way back on it. For there, you always are – arms wide open and full of forgiveness and love. Forever my light in the darkness. Forever my compass, my peace, and my hope.

"Search me and know my heart, test me and know my thoughts, point out anything that offends you and lead me along the path of everlasting life." Psalms 139:24-25

"He has shown you, what is good and what is required: to do justly, to love mercy, and to walk humbly with our God."

Table of Contents

Introduction 11

The Song 13

Alwind's House 33

Mountain Doors of Cedars 69

Just a Knock 95

The Wizard and His many 103

The Secret 127

The Task 139

Epilogue 148

Introduction

This story has no specific date in time, but instead takes place in a land that could be here or in a different world entirely. Instead, this story deals with the reality of here and everywhere. Light and darkness. Good and Evil. This story follows a family and a journey they are led to go on whether they were ready for it or not. Each family member has strengths and weaknesses that help or get in the way. Throughout this story you will see that it will take much more than this book to finish this adventure. But for now, get a blanket, get comfy and dive into this story about family, friendship, light and darkness.

Chapter 1

The Song

If you looked across the lands of the world, one would simply say there was a time when it was lighter, beautiful, and filled with activity. But not now. Darkness had settled over the lands; it was quickly growing stronger and pushing away any light that took the day. Whatever direction you roamed, it was quite gray and eerie, and greeting one's neighbor had been gone for quite some time. Shadows, hurried steps, screams and worried whispers, endless hunger pains gripped most people who kept to the shadows. It was quite hopeless, the world. But in the west lands, there was a family. They stayed on the path of light and took in the light of the day when it appeared. They were not afraid; they were able to keep farming their land as they built by the path. Seeing those that stayed on the path of light knew a secret many had forgotten. But it was there that you could hear the forgotten sound of children laughing, or a mother singing, for the songs and laughter had mostly vanished. But in the west lands, where the mountains still stood strong and forests wound round and round, on a tiny piece of land called West Meadow, was Alwind's favorite Family of Seven. It was bedtime and as always at bedtime, if you walked by, you would hear a soft clear voice singing to her children Alwind's Tale:

Alwind's Tale

Above the clouds
Above our lands
Above the dark and evil hands
Hear my child in this song
The secret hope that can be found
Follow down
The narrow path
Run my child
Do not look back
The shield of light
It will protect you
Run my child
Run to the mountain

To the Doors of Cedars

Seek the truth
And you will find
Which door to take
Which door is right
With just a knock
It will be opened
With good intentions
Or you'll be forbidden

Look for the ancient words
Inscribed on the Ancient tree
From birth you will have
known them
Read them right for
They must be spoken
If you are worthy
The gift will be given
Beware of yourself
use only when right
Or it will be taken
For it holds the secret light
That will send away
The Wizard and his many
And reveal what is hidden
Hush my child
You must Listen
Hush my child
You must Listen

> Follow the whisper
> Watch out for the Wizard
> Follow the whisper
> And help will come
> from the Armor Giver
> Yes, help will come
> From the Armor Giver...

"Sing it again Mama," the children begged. Their mother smiled. Sean, Kayleigh, Hugh, Fiona and Liam snuggled in the big bed their daddy made from the strong cedar trees that grew around their home. They loved the evenings when their Mama would sing Alwind's Tale to them and share the special words she had grown up learning.

"Alright but this time you must try to sing it all with me," said Mama. And so, they sang together. Sean, 11; Kayleigh, 10; Hugh almost 9; Fiona 5; and Liam 4 all sang loudly with their Mama when all of a sudden, a booming voice joined them at the end:

"FROM THE ARMOR GIVER!!!!!!!!!!!!!!!!!!" Multiple notes were shouted out in the end by Papa, who had just come in from a long day of getting supplies.

"Papa!!!" Wild screams of delight took place as Papa threw the littles in the air and tickled them till they couldn't breathe. He then wrestled with the older three till they too couldn't breathe from laughing so hard. Mama joined in the laughter as she began to warm Papa's food.

"Ok children back in bed. Are you ready for the Ancient words?"

"Yes, Mama, we are ready."

Mama smiled and said, "Tonight it's Papa's turn to share the ancient words."

Papa faced the children and softly spoke: "The light is found through the narrow gate; not made for all but few. But the darkness, however, is broad, wide and easy, so many will follow through. Though the gate to the light is very narrow, filled with a difficult road and hard at times to find this is the road to life, the road to the Armor Giver. The wise will follow the straight path that requires work and strong heart. Fools will follow the widened paths and it all will lead to wrought. Beware of the Wizard and his many. A disguise of the right but his actions prove dark. Beware of the Wizard and his many."

The embers crackled as the kids listened silently to their fathers' words. The Ancient words. Mama and Papa from the first day of Sean's birth had repeated these words to him. But Sean knew they were important. For they always asked the children to repeat them over and over. He loved listening to his parents share these ancient sayings, but a part of him wondered these days why they were so important. As the eldest, he was expected to practice these sayings when he would take his brothers and sisters outside to play during the few hours that sunlight came upon the land. Sean blew on the embers and watched them grow brighter as he added another log into the fire. He sighed and turned back his attention to his father who was explaining to the little ones the words.

"Ok children," Mom smiled as she continued, "It's time for bed."

Once the children were tucked in safely, Mama sat by Papa as he ate his dinner.

"Any change Love?" she asked.

"Yes Love, but not the change we were hoping for. The Wizard grows stronger. He heads this way. The light grows shorter and shorter. Darkness has taken over beyond the cedar trees. There is no daylight there, just darkness and much sadness. I hear them cry but I cannot do much. Not even the rocks will spark light there. We must send the children soon. They must get to him sooner. We have less time than we were hoping for my Love." He said gently and sadly.

Mama sat quietly. She put her hand into her husband's strong hand. She always felt safer when holding it. She could see for herself the light was fading into the shadows and becoming less and less. She barely had time to dry the clothes these days. As the darkness grew stronger the Ancient words weakened as fewer and fewer were keeping them in their heart.

"We must ask Alwind what to do." Mama said.

"Yes, yes, tomorrow even. We must all visit him. We must bring his favorite bread and figs with honey." Papa said smiling.

"Oh yes, dear Alwind. He would be sad if I didn't bring those. I know someone else who likes bread with figs and honey." winked Mama. "I will make that first when I rise, Love. Then we should go once it is ready."

Papa nodded in agreement and said, "I saw another one today, in our Cedar forest. He would not come with me. He would not try to eat the food I gave him. He sat and cried and held his knees. He looked like our Sean boy's age. I tried everything. But he would not move into the lighted path. Broke my heart love; they chose to stay in the shadowland. When I said the Ancient words, the boy looked up, but his eyes were completely grey; all the color and life had gone, no color came back as I said the words, instead he covered his ears and screamed. The ancient words are being ignored more and more. I fear there may be very few of us left now…." Papa let a tear fall and then sniffed loudly and cleared his throat. He set his jaw tight, looked down at Mama and smiled; and lightly let his fingers fall through her beautiful long hair.

Mama put her head on Papa's shoulder to tell him she understood his sadness. She felt sorry for the people of the shadowlands. They could not remember the words. They sat in the shadows crying and in agony. They couldn't even eat when she would try to feed the lost ones that would stumble into the forest. But the lighted path scared them as well and they would not follow her like some would before. More and more seemed terrified of the Ancient Words. She remembered when they used to bring comfort and relief.

Only one other neighbor had kept the Ancient words to heart. Their dear old friend Alwind. Alwind would tell them what they must do. For soon, the Wizard would pass through the Cedar trees and be upon them. He was determined to fill the lands of the world with darkness.

Alwind was old. He had watched many forget the Ancient words. He tried to share with all who moved into the lands. He often traveled sharing them around the distant lands. But lately he always returned discouraged; often chased by the Wizard's many; and sometimes even injured by the ones that lived in the shadows. He always found encouragement in the "Family of Seven". Actually, His favorite Family of Seven, he would smile and say.

Chapter 2

The Family of Seven

"Sean boy and Kayleigh girl, wake up my loves. Please get the younger three ready. We journey to Alwind's place today. Mama is busy making bread and honey figs. She needs your help while she prepares food for the day and gets the house ready for our leave. I need to let the animals out to roam while we are away. Make sure to pack a few clothes, we may stay there for a while." said Papa.

"Yes Papa!" They half-said and half-yawned.

Sean rubbed his eyes and stretched out his arms. He felt like he could sleep maybe 5 hours more. It was still dark outside. Was it morning or night? He couldn't tell these days. The light was coming and going quicker than before. He sniffed and smiled. He loved the smell of Mama's fresh bread, and the sizzle of the figs Mama was roasting till they burst open. She then drizzled them with golden honey and served them with homemade cheese she made with tiny specks of sage.

Sean turned and started to gently push Hugh's shoulder. He liked being the eldest. He was almost as tall as Mama and he liked the fact that his parents counted on him for help. He also loved to tease his brothers and sisters about being the eldest, therefore in charge, perhaps even when Mama and Papa didn't need him to be in charge. Sean had golden hair with light blue eyes. He loved to learn new things. Quite handsome, his smile was large and infectious. He was tall when he stood up straight, but he tended to be slightly hunched over – usually thinking about something or sketching out a plan he had. Often, lost in his thoughts, he would sometimes forget about chores. But he always was willing to help and would rush to do what he forgot apologetically when reminded. He loved working with Papa and had a gift for memorizing things he was told or things that he read. He often was hardest on himself. But he also was the quickest to forgive. He loved music. Well, he loved playing music. He could play the guitar, and the little wooden pipe Papa had made for him. Mama loved it when he would play for the family around the fire at night. He secretly enjoyed playing too. It took his mind off the darkness settling around them. But back to waking up the others.

"Ok brother…. I tried gently. You asked for it!!!! HUGH!!!" yelled Sean as he jumped onto his brother and started tickling him.

Hugh yelled out and then started laughing as he realized it was only Sean. His bright green eyes grew big to match his smile as he punched his brother in the arm as hard as he could to get him back. Sean rubbed his arm and told his brother to get dressed as he moved on to his other siblings. Hugh didn't realize it, but he was the strongest of the five. He had a small stout build with muscles already formed. When it came to activity, he always gave more effort and energy than anyone else. But only if it interested him. Otherwise, sure enough, you'd find him hiding, somewhere to avoid doing his chores. Being a middle child wasn't always easy but there was always one advantage. Each child knew Hugh was the best to play with, and Hugh was always ready to play. They also went to him when they were scared. Hugh was never afraid to face danger. He wasn't afraid of the darkness when they'd walk through the forest and drop something off the path. Hugh was always the first to volunteer to go get what fell off the path. His parents watched in amazement and sometimes with worry as he would run as fast as he could and bravely pick up the item in the darkness and run back happily.

Hugh stretched and scratched his head; he sat up quickly once he smelled Mama's food sizzling on the stove. He started to get dressed but not before throwing a pillow at his sister Kayleigh, interrupting Sean's attempt to tell Kayleigh to get up and help him with the babies.

"Hugh!" laughed Kayleigh. Sweet Kayleigh. She knew Mama needed help, so rather than play she quickly got dressed. She pulled back her long, beautiful light brown hair, smoothed down her dress to make sure it was straight and went right into the kitchen. Her light brown eyes often had flecks of gold which you could see when she smiled but at that moment, she was focused on helping her Mama. Tall and slender, she moved gracefully like a ballerina. Without even asking, she went outside to fill the kettle with water from their well and put the kettle on the stove. She checked the fire inside the oven to make sure it was keeping hot for Mama. She brought Mama the eggs and started cutting bread to toast and butter. Mama smiled gratefully at Kayleigh and stopped to hug her. Kayleigh was dependable and one who always saw the good in people. She was the quietest of the five. She was always thinking of ways to help others. From making the big bed in secret or making tea for Papa and Mama as a surprise. When the babies got hurt playing outside, they cried to Kayleigh, and she would bring them to Mama and help dress their wounds. At night she often sang to the babies until they fell asleep. They loved her like a second mom. Kayleigh would often let Mama and Papa sleep in on their day of rest and would bake bread, cook the eggs and make a little salad of fruit drizzled with honey. She loved cooking and creating new things to eat just like her Mama. Everyone's bellies especially loved it when Kayleigh would make a new dish. Each sibling usually volunteers to taste test first or lick the bowl or spoon to "help".

"Kayleigh, can you help me get the babies ready?" asked Sean, "I need to go outside and help Papa get the house ready for our journey. We're going to Alwind's house!"

Kayleigh nodded and smiled. She loved visiting Alwind. He always played games and told stories from the ancient words. She rushed to get ready herself to let the babies sleep a little longer. She then gently went to Fiona first. She tickled her, moved Fiona's dark wild hair out of her face, and whispered in her ear their plans to go to Alwind's.

Fiona opened one eye and then the other. She giggled with laughter. Her lips and cheeks turned instantly rose red and her green eyes grew big with wonder. Her wild black wavy hair framed her face. Fiona stretched dramatically and sighed a heavy sigh. She then danced across the floor and picked out her favorite dress. Fiona was always ready to dress up and go somewhere. She loved people. She often grew sad as more and more people grew afraid of them. When they'd walk through the forest, she would try her best to cheer them up; singing a song Mama taught her or dancing around them. But more and more of them would not follow Mama to their path. They'd cover their ears and just cry. But Alwind! She couldn't wait to see Alwind. He would throw her in the air and teach her new songs. Fiona was the child that would cry with others and get upset if another brother or sister got in trouble. Fiona was also the more dramatic child. Her eyes always grew big as she told stories around the fire at night and the family would sit and giggle with laughter as her tales were often wild and full of spirit. She was beautiful like a delicate doll, but wild like an untamed stallion. She hated brushing her hair but even with it tangled and wild she looked so pretty. She was called their sunshine girl. For she brought joy and sunshine as she danced around so carefree.

Kayleigh saw Fiona was fine playing on her bed with her baby doll, telling her of their journey, so she bent down and scooped Liam out of bed. She gave him a kiss and rocked him for a couple of minutes. Liam, blonde, brown hair and chubby cheeks, smiled and stretched. He sniffed and immediately opened his grey-blue eyes and asked his sister, "Kayleigh!" Is it time to eat?"

Kayleigh laughed and told Liam he had to get ready first for the day and that they were going to see Alwind today. Liam screeched with excitement. Kayleigh picked out his clothes as Liam excitedly threw his clothes off of himself and ran around naked as little four-year-old's do. Liam was strong and stubborn. He waved at Kayleigh to shoo her when she tried to help him with his socks. He was determined to do it himself as long as someone was beside him. Although, if he got hurt, he wanted his Mama right away. Food was his favorite thing in the world. Too busy to pay attention, Liam was also their accident-prone child. Walking sideways or backwards often to say something to one of his siblings, he would find himself walking right into something or someone. Thankfully he had a mighty strong head on his shoulders, and it often had bumps on it. So, Liam got a lot of attention from Mama or Kayleigh as bumps happened often. But his encouraging words and incredible hugs were so appreciated and needed by all. He loved to be praised and hated corrections. But always, Liam was ready to be loved and to give love.

"Ok, I'm ready. Is it time to eat now please!" whined Liam

"Good morning, Liam", Mama said, "Yes, it's time to eat. But first I need my Liam hug and then come sit down honey!" Liam smiled wide and wrapped his arm around his Mama as she bent down, and they gave each other a big, long squeeze. He then quickly sat down and picked up a piece of warm bread.

"Oh Mama, thank you so much for cooking! Everything looks yummy. I know it will be yummy. It's always yummy! Thank you, Kayleigh, for helping me get dressed so I can eat!" Liam quickly said. Liam was their encourager. He gave compliments constantly without even knowing he was doing it. Each person could count on Liam to say "Oh wow! Good job" or "That's so nice" or "That's so yummy!"

The family sat together and sang the Ancient song of thanks:
Oh, Giver of daily bread
Oh, Giver of Life
For this day we thank you
For what is ahead we give to you
Thank you for another day
Thank you for our family
Oh, Giver we are truly thankful to you.

Over eggs, tea, toast and fruit, Papa talked about their trip to see Alwind. The older children knew it would be long because they didn't often go to see Alwind. Usually, Alwind came to them. In fact, this would only be the babies second time. Papa reminded them they must stick to the lighted path and that part of the journey this time would be in darkness as the daylight had shortened quite a bit since their last visit.

After breakfast, the older children helped Mama pack up food and bags for the journey. It seemed like they were taking more clothes and food than usual, but they didn't think to ask about that. They were too excited to go.

Mama looked around the kitchen and bedroom to make sure she had everything. Mama had long dark brown wavy hair, light brown eyes, and smiled often. She was also very sensible about what to wear. Fiona would often scold Mama for not wearing her nice dress. But Mama would laugh and explain that she did not have time to wear a fancy dress. The children loved

The Amor Giver

their Mama. Mama was always going through a list in her head of what tasks needed to be done. But she often paused to play a small game of chase or would pull aside a child to play a game of stones and sticks or to teach them something new. She often looked out into the distance. She loved to talk about the Armor Giver and the beauty of what was given all around them. Her favorite thing to do was to watch the children laugh with their Papa just before bed as she would sit and sip her tea. She felt a strong arm on her shoulder and knew it was Papa. She looked into his sea-blue eyes and nodded. She was ready for their journey. She had a feeling deep down that it would be some time before she ever returned to this beautiful home they created together. She wondered if this was the last time she'd see it, so she inhaled the smells of home one last time, kissed Papa on the cheek and headed outside to the children.

Papa smiled. He could always count on Mama to bring him some comfort. Not that he ever indicated that he needed it. Papa was strong, tall and loved to solve problems. He loved building and farming. He loved the sweat that would come with the hard work and hard hours. It would be his assurance that he did his best and had put in a full day. It was hard to know by the daylight anymore if one put in a full day, as the darkness was expanding and taking over. Papa was quiet but often deep in thought. He loved to laugh with the children and when he'd see the worry across Mama's face, his favorite accomplishment was to do whatever it took to make her laugh. Even if that meant making a fool of himself. He loved Mama and the children deeply. He was determined to protect them with all he had. He knew Alwind would know what to do. He locked the door and looked out toward Mama and the children. He sighed and knew deep down they would not be returning. The darkness was coming. It was growing stronger. They needed to get to Alwind as soon as possible.

Everyone lifted their hooded coats to blend with the others, especially Mama and Papa. Most people covered themselves, or hid behind cloaks, not wanting to be seen. It was not like before when one wanted to know their neighbor. People stayed hidden now, suspicious of one another. This was actually a relief for Mama and Papa as they were not wanting to stand out these days. And especially today, they did not want their difference to be noticed. Today was not a day to stop and help a stranger. For up close someone could see that Mama and Papa had markings different than many in their land. They had a special line of symbols etched into the crown of their heads. In fact, the children didn't notice it, as it blended well, but the Wizard was after these kinds and Mama and Papa knew this. They could not take the chance of it being noticed. But that is for a little later. All the children knew was that away from home, this is how they dressed.

Mama and Papa pulled their hoods forward to cover their faces a bit more. They looked around their land once more. Everyone strapped a bag of items they had packed to their backs. Fiona was in charge of her little dolly and Liam was in charge of his wooden carved boat. They looked to the path that led to Alwind's house and started on. Mama led them on the path and started singing Alwind's Tale and the children excitedly followed not noticing the concern on Papa's face as he walked last to make sure the children were between him and Mama. Papa hoped that the light would last for most of the trip.

Chapter 3

Alwind's House

It was still dark when the family of seven had left for Alwind's house. They walked together and sang Alwind's tale together and then Mama and Papa took turns sharing the Ancient words and having the children repeat them. After a while, Sean whistled and the younger ones carefully listened, racing to guess the song. As they walked down the path, they crossed with a few strangers, none of whom they knew. The strangers were often in a hurry and passed them off the path. They looked scared and hungry but also determined to get away from the sun that was shining down on them. Mama and Papa would always look ahead and tell the children to look down and be quiet when they would see a stranger. You never knew if it could be one of the Wizard's many, who held dark magic within them. But so far this path has been clear of them. The shadow people were the ones who gave in to the Wizard and his many, but they were still human. They often forgot their neighbors and the ancient words which had brought happiness and peace throughout the land years and years ago. Instead, they would grumble and grunt and look frantically for something but yet not know what it was. They were lost. Mama and Papa would usually try to help them or bring the ones that wanted help to Alwind, but not today. Today they needed to see Alwind as fast as possible. So, Mama would leave bread off the path, and the children could sometimes hear behind them someone snatch up the bread and make terrible noises as they gobbled up the bread as fast as they could.

They did not stop to rest. When Fiona and Liam grew tired, Mama and Papa took turns carrying them. Sean knew this journey must be important because his whistling stopped, and he took Liam from Papa after a few hours and put Liam on his back. Liam squealed with happiness as he rode on his big brother's back. Papa then took Fiona and put her on his shoulders to give Mama's back a rest. Mama took out some bread and stuffed each piece with two dates. They ate as they walked. By mid- afternoon the clouds started to form, and a mist of darkness began to fill the skies.

Off in the distance though, Papa could see the mountain where Alwind's house was. He could see the carving of the Cedar tree on the mountain edge. It would be another hour before they were there. Papa smiled and decided to make it a game. Perhaps if they raced to the mountain a bit by playing tag, they might not be climbing up the steep path in the total darkness.

"Tag Mama!!" laughed Papa and he started to run. Mama smirked and ran towards Hugh, who was too fast for Mama and ran past Papa not looking back. The babies shrieked with laughter and ran as well. The game lasted for a half-hour before they all began to tire. The sky was getting darker. The children did not like the darkness. They noticed it was not as bright and held each other's hands. Sean took Liam's and Kayleigh took Fiona's. Hugh bravely walked ahead of Papa.

"Ok children, the light is going earlier tonight than before. But we need not be afraid. Remember the ancient words about darkness?

"The darkness fears the most you see
For just a spark will make it flee
The Wizard loves the dark to play
He steals the light
But don't dismay
The one who made the light is stronger
So, fear not child
Though dark grows longer
Have faith for light will always come

And just a spark will light all dark"

The children rose a little higher as they said those words. No longer afraid as the light was fading. They knew what would come next. Those noises. Those horrible noises. They sounded like frightened coyotes that had been left by their parents to find food. The sound is eerie, and you can tell they are shrieks filled with terror. But the noises were coming from humans; people full of fear and shrieking like coyotes. It was hard to hear, but somehow remembering the ancient words made them feel stronger and braver. They followed Papa and, just as the light was fading, Mama took a strip of cotton cloth and tied it to each of their wrists. They would climb the mountain tied together. Papa looked up the steep path and started to climb the almost sheered-off steps up to Alwind's. Papa knew the hardest would be at the top. They would need to climb for a bit before that part though. Hopefully they would not give Alwind a fright. It was a long way down. Papa would lift Hugh and Sean up so they could help pull the others up and then Papa would climb the rest himself. Just as he was about to lift Hugh up, a stick suddenly came about an inch from Papa's face and a booming voice shouted:

"Are you friend of light or foe?"

Papa laughed and shouted "Alwind, you almost scared me off this mountain! Friend of light silly man! Now help me get the children off this steep path so they don't tumble down with me!"

"Oh!!", howled Alwind with joy, "It's my favorite family of seven!!! Oh, I had a feeling I would see you soon. In fact, I have checked every day at this same time the last few weeks. Come on children. Come to old Alwind."

One by one the children jumped onto Alwind and gave him a big hug. Hugh showed Alwind he lost another tooth and Sean showed Alwind he was almost as tall as his mother now. Alwind's heart was so happy to see them.

Alwind was tall and had white hair and dark tanned skin. Alwind was old but not so old to chase the children and hold them on his lap. He was almost 67. "That's almost 70!" he would say proudly. He always had his walking stick with beautiful carvings etched into the dark stained cedar wood. The carvings were not ordinary. They were square shapes that spiraled up the large stick. Within each square were detailed carvings of pictures. Each carving had a story to it. From the bottom carving which held the story of how time began, to the very top of the walking stick which held Alwind's favorite truth story, the end of the evil Wizard's reign and the Armor Giver's return. Alwind was given this walking stick as a gift from his wife. She knew how he loved to share the Ancient words with all he met. The beautiful stick would often start the conversations for him as people would admire the carvings and ask what they meant. He especially loved sharing these true stories with children. They always made story telling fun. The children loved to sit by the fire and hear Alwind tell these ancient stories. Wherever Alwind went, his walking stick was with him.

His smile filled his face, and his laugh was deep and loud. Tonight, the children didn't notice Alwind's furrowed brow as he turned to look around them. Mama put her hand on Alwind's shoulder, and he turned back and smiled at her. Then Alwind's eyes widened with excitement as Mama whispered what she brought - his favorite dish; roasted figs with honey, Mama's bread and her hand made cheese. The horrible sounds began to ring out and Alwind rushed them inside and closed the door where the light was bright, and they could talk.

Papa breathed a sigh of relief as Alwind closed the door.

"Just in time my dear friend. I was beginning to worry when weeks had passed and there was no sign of you and your family." whispered Alwind

"Yes, Alwind. I've been planning to visit you friend. I should have brought us earlier but was trying to prepare the land and animals. When I realized how the darkness was taking over quicker than I had planned, I decided it was time. I just didn't think it would happen this fast. I was very worried today. The noises grow louder, and the darkness grows longer. We don't have much time do we Alwind?" Papa took a deep breath.

"Aye. Not much time but we have hope. Let's enjoy some rest tonight and I will certainly sit down right now and enjoy this lovely feast you brought me."

"Come my favorite family of seven! Sit down, I have just made some veggie and lentil stew and found some berries and seeds today. Let's eat! But first, let's give thanks!"

And so, they sang with Alwind the Ancient song of thanks:

"Oh, Giver of daily bread
Oh, Giver of Life
For this day we thank you
For what is ahead we give to you
Thank you for another day
Thank you for our family
Oh, Giver we are truly thankful to you."

They ended the night around the lamp of light Alwind had made. It was about two feet long with seven wicks. It brightened up the cave. They pulled thick blankets around them and listened as Alwind shared the Ancient story. He pointed to the bottom of his staff where there was carved a shape of the world:

"Long ago the Armor Giver made the land we live in. He filled the days with light and evenings even had light from the moon. He filled the land with only good things. He created beings like himself but not in wisdom. He loved these beings and created a wonderful world for them. But He also wanted these beings to know him and to have the freedom to choose to love him. And to do this, there had to be one that was not like him. One that would be the opposite of him. And so, the Armor Giver created the Wizard with the choice to choose good or evil. The Armor Giver tried to show the Wizard why the light was good, why his ways were best. He gave him every chance to choose the right path, but he gave him freedom to choose the opposite. At first the Wizard loved learning from the Armor Giver but sadly the Wizard preferred darkness and immediately began taking beings away from the Armor Giver, making beings doubt in the love of the Armor Giver, making them question His ways and the light. His power was strong like the Armor Giver's but there was no love in that power. But there are a few of us who keep to the Armor Giver's way. We trust in his ancient words. For there is a saying that one day the Armor Giver will come and fight the Wizard and his many. And those of us who remain true to the Ancient words will be there alongside Him in the final battle. But the Wizard does not know these words and he does not know the ending. Do you want to know the ending children?

The children nodded yes frantically and leaned forward in anticipation.

"Though the Wizard will grow the darkness
Though many will follow in the shadows
He will be kept from the hidden
Those that are true will find the pieces
The Armor they will need to fight by His side
The side of the Armor Giver will rise
And the secret will unfold
To the horror of the Wizard
Because it may not seem so

No, it may not seem so
But down he will go with his many
And the light will burst forth destroying his darkness
And they that stay true
Will reign with the Armor Giver"

Papa and Mama smiled at each other as the kids stared at Alwind in wonder. Could it be true that this would all end well? Papa and Mama hoped with all their heart and felt a warmth fill them up that told them it was true.

"Alwind, is it true the Wizard was handsome?" asked Fiona.

"Was the Wizard really smarter than the other Awe-bearers? He doesn't seem very smart." Hugh said.

"Don't be fooled children, the Wizard is very cunning. But that is different than being wise. Sadly, the Wizard is the most foolish, yet his story didn't start that way. Would you like one more bedtime story children?" asked Alwind looking at their parents really quick for approval.

"Yes!!!" all 5 shouted.

"Sometimes I wonder if his story needs to be told, but I think it wise to share the Wizard's story. Let us dive into the beginning children. The Wizard was the most handsome creature created, ever. He stood a head taller than all the other heavenly creatures. Giants came to be because of him. He, and beings like him, had forms they could shift into, but only to serve mankind.

To give messages, or to help. Their natural being was giant in size, taller than cedar trees. Their arms and legs were covered in wing-like shapes, and they had wings from their shoulders that allowed them to fly. These beings had pear-like scales all over their wings that had an eye in each scale and their pupils were a beautiful gold. As the wings would move the eyes would close and only open when they were still. They were the watchers over the world. The Wizard was the leader of these watchers. His skin was a brilliant pearl color that shimmered and often looked golden as the lights reflected off his skin. He was the handsomest and most powerful of the beings. He shined so brightly, and all created looked up to him for he was given the privilege of walking with the Armor Giver and learning all that the Armor Giver did. The Armor Giver called the Wizard into the highest position. He showed the Wizard compassion, treating him as a son, mentoring him. The Armor Giver showed him how he had made the animals and taught him how to use minerals He had created to make tools, and how to bring nutrients into the soil to produce the tastiest fruits and vegetables. He put him in charge of the Awe-bearers or watchers that would care for the earth and all that lived within it. He put him in charge of teaching these Awe-bearers how to help the humans, and animals, and lands live peacefully and joyfully. He walked the earth freely and could walk into the heavens just as quickly to give an update to the Armor Giver. The Armor Giver also loved to join his creation on earth. Taking on the form of man to show humanity how to care for the animals and each other. He even let the humans name the animals. This puzzled the Wizard as he found humans to be beneath him and felt annoyed that the Armor Giver would waste time on them and give them a privilege, he thought he should have been given. He kept these thoughts hidden though and began making excuses to not join the Armor Giver in his walks with the humans. Instead, he would spy on their interactions and his jealousy grew as he could see the Armor Giver loved these things very much. They were not like him, they were not like the Awe-bearers, they were not even close in wisdom to others. He had no trouble sharing these thoughts with the Awe-bearers under his care. The Wizard shined brightest, like a star, and the Awe-bearers below him admired him, and secretly he began to relish all the attention. He found the Awe-bearers in his care easily influenced and his pride grew as he knew he could easily influence their minds. He liked this power and longed for it to grow. He then found his interactions with the Armor Giver boring and annoying as the Armor Giver tried teaching him the importance of love, of care, of patience, of teaching so that these humans could grow slowly in wisdom and knowledge so they would stay humble. The Wizard wanted them to know everything right away so he could influence them just as he was influencing the awe-bearers he was teaching. He looked often at himself and smiled at His beauty and light.

But if anyone had been paying attention, they would have noticed his light began to fade. Soon the Wizard found it painful to be close to the Armor Giver. The Armor Giver's light began hurting the Wizard's eyes. He'd choose to be with the other creatures that were made instead. And instead of doing what the Armor Giver wanted him to do, he started questioning him secretly to his followers and those he was in charge of. The Wizard began showing favoritism and took interest in ones that seemed quite loyal to him. One in particular he decided to rename "Creature". Creature felt special while the others nervously looked around because only the Creator had the right to name what He made in the heavens – it was against the order of above to assume the role of the Creator. The wizard had decided he knew better. He started using his gifts the Armor Giver had given him to distort and change what was already made. With every misuse of power – the light from the wizard faded. His eyes grew a grey film that took away its brilliance. He was able to hide it through magic, but it was only a mask. A reflection or glimpse from a mirror would reveal his true look. Even then the Armor Giver invited the Wizard to walk with him and learn from him. He would ask the Wizard to share his thoughts – but Wizard smiled blindly and would hide His evil plotting. He acted as if He was loyal to the Armor Giver. But that was a lie. He tried to hide his fading light by staying away from reflective elements and started morphing himself into different beings so that he could roam freely without being noticed by the

Armor Giver's mighty warrior awe-bearers, Gabriel and Michael, nosy beings in the Wizard's mind. They seemed overly concerned about him and would not give in to him when he'd question the Armor Giver's choices. They stood loyal – he hated them!

One day the Wizard was sneaking around as a 4-legged serpent when he saw the first man and woman looking at the trees that the Armor Giver had given to them to admire and to eat. But he caught the woman glancing at the tree of Wisdom. The tree he wanted them to eat from though the Armor Giver had not given them permission to eat. He wanted them to see that he, not the Armor Giver, could show them a better way to live…. well actually he wanted them to understand him better so he could take over earth and build his own kingdom. He remembered the woman's glance and decided to make a few more visits before interacting with the humans again.

The Wizard began visiting the woman. Speaking kindly and complimenting her beauty and how special she was to be able to walk and learn from the Armor Giver. He then began to use the words of the Armor Giver in a twisted way. Asking her questions about what the Armor Giver said but twisting the truth enough to make her wonder if she heard right. Man did not help his wife remember the Ancient Words. They took for granted the words and did not let them be known well enough. The fruit from the forbidden tree began to look so delicious. How could a bite of food really bring any harm the Wizard whispered? He began to whisper more lies with each visit. He said that the Amor Giver was keeping them from secret wisdom and knowledge to prevent the man and woman from being like the Armor Giver; powerful and all-knowing. The Armor Giver had been devoted to them and had given them so much freedom and happiness, they instead grew greedy and obsessed over the one thing He asked them to not possess. With just a bite, humankind fell for the Wizard's trickery.

This immediately broke the relationship between heaven and earth. The Wizard took with him his loyal Awe-bearer, named "Creature", and he took many more Awe-bearers. They lost their names, their eyes grew colorless, darkened and distorted, and they became creatures filled with dark magic and power. They enjoyed this power and enjoyed serving the Wizard. They believed they could build a better kingdom under the Wizard. They, the created, thought they could do better than the Armor Giver! And so, the Wizard and his many have roamed and ruled the earth. They desire to bring man and woman away from the Armor Giver. They taught man and woman how to make weapons, how to use darkness to increase in number, how to betray and lie, how to crave power, how to use magic to gain control; and sadly, how to pull away from the calling of the Armor Giver. The Wizard hates light, he grows the darkness. But there are some who have fought against the Wizard and his many and continue to pass this secret on. The Wizard and his many know the world is cursed and it is their kingdom, but they are trying to slow down the spread of the good news – that there is a new kingdom arriving soon, a battle that will end the power of the Wizard. They have but one goal – to build the kingdom of darkness, to bring man and woman into the shadows and cut short man's and woman's chance to know the Armor Giver. Wars, famines, hardships, greed, etc. All these tools the Wizard has put in mans' hands to use to his advantage. But there is hope for humankind. There is hope in those that fight against the Wizard and his many. For as they fight, the light keeps on. And where there is light – the Armor Giver will be found!"

"Hurray!!!" yelled Liam. Giggles abounded and Alwind shouted a Hurray himself.

"Ok children off to bed! I need to talk with your Mama and Papa. We must do a lot of preparing to leave in two days' time."

"Night Mama and Papa! Night Alwind! Thank you for sharing the Ancient words tonight. Come on Fiona and Liam, I'll help you get ready for bed." said Kayleigh. Hugh raced past Kayleigh and the little ones to get ready and claim his favorite spot. He giggled as he went by.

Sean looked at Alwind and stood there for a moment, quiet, yet wanting to ask something.

"Yes Sean, you want to ask me something. What is it?" Alwind kindly asked.

Sean turned a little pink and said, "Alwind, these ancient words we memorize and these stories, how can

I know it's all true. You and Mama and Papa seem so sure. But how Alwind? I really want to believe."

Alwind smiled and gently pulled Sean to sit by him.

"Sean, how do you feel when the light is around us?"

"I don't know how to quite explain it, but I guess I feel like all is right with the world. I feel a warmth in my heart. I feel a happiness I can't describe. Why?"

"Well Sean, how do you feel when the darkness comes?"

"Hmm, I feel sad, and I guess to be honest I feel a bit scared and alone. I don't like it. I wish it would go away and I don't want it to grow."

"Yes Sean, that is the right way to feel about the darkness. It was never meant to grow. The Armor Giver wanted us to choose him, to always choose him. But he wanted us to truly choose him. Sadly, many chose the Wizard's side. But you my boy – you love the light. You see its importance. That is the first step, and you are learning the ancient words which will help you know the Armor Giver better. And one day my boy, He will speak to you. One day. You will see him, and you will never be the same again. Just like me, just like your Mama and Papa. And he will give you a gift. A gift that can never be taken. It will show that you belong to his side. But that is for another time. Off to bed you go."

Sean nodded and felt better. He hugged his Mama and Papa and slipped into bed. Hugh turned to face him and asked "Sean do you think that's all true, I mean

Alwind is so old and a little crazy. Do you think what he shares with us is true?"

Sean said seriously, "Hugh, quit eaves dropping all the time and stop calling Alwind crazy. You like the light more than dark too, don't you?"

Hugh said matter-of-factly, "I like both. I'm not scared of either.... unlike You!" Sean punched him in the arm and then they both giggled. Papa looked over to them and they knew it was time to sleep. These two loved to tease each other but deep down knew they'd be there for each other till the end.

All was quiet as the lamp light began to fade. Only three stayed up late into the night whispering and planning their journey on the narrow path. Two days would pass quickly.

Chapter 4

Keep the Path!

Alwind and his favorite Family of Seven slowly climbed down the mountain. Alwind, 66 plus years young, was not as quick as he used to be, but he was strong. Taller than the family, he was able to climb easily up and down his mountain. Though he was skin and bones from living alone for so many years. He looked back at his mountain and smiled. He and his beloved Teresa had built that home together. No children of their own yet many saw them as parents.

They poured into families who followed the Ancient Words. It has been ten years without her. He missed her everyday but would often talk aloud to her as if she was in the room with him. Mama and Papa missed her too. She was often the one who would remind Alwind to eat and to sleep. While Alwind would share the Ancient stories and words, Teresa would quietly be cooking or serving tea to all who would listen. She too would often share the ancient words to those in the shadow. One day while on the path she saw a child about to be killed by his parents, for all that was right in the world had gone. She went off the path and the Wizard was nearby. Wizard sent his Creature into the parents and as she pushed the child out of the way, the shadow dwellers killed Teresa instead of the boy. The boy ran away and eventually he ran onto the straight path. He saw that as he stayed on the path the darkness stayed just behind him. He ran and ran till he fell on the path and fell asleep. Alwind was looking for Teresa, calling her name when he stumbled onto the child. Alwind asked the child if he had seen his wife and described her. Teresa always wore a yellow scarf. The boy's eyes widened, and he shook his head yes. He told Alwind what happened and Alwind told the boy to stay. Alwind ran and ran till he found his beloved Teresa. He covered her body with her beautiful scarf and carried her back to their mountain where he buried her. He took the little boy and cared for him, putting medicine on the wounds his parents had given him and sharing the ancient words to help heal the internal wounds that he had been given. He then brought him to a family in the North that he trusted, hoping this boy would choose the Armor Giver as well. So many came to visit Alwind to say goodbye to Teresa. Alwind promised her he would try to save many more children and families.

He had a feeling he wouldn't be seeing his mountain for a long while. The darkness grew stronger, and the cunning Wizard was growing tired of the safe path. He made sure to send his many and Creature as close to the path as they could to spy on any who would walk it. He had to make sure his favorite Family of Seven got to the Armor Giver before Creature got its claws on any of them. He didn't tell the others but if anyone had opened Alwind's pack, they would have caught a glimpse of yellow in there. Again, the darkness lingered longer than it would have just days before. The air was colder and dryer. They had slept on the path but luckily there were some large stones put on the path. Everyone woke up wanting water. Thankfully a brook ran along the narrow path. Mama and Hugh went together to fill the water pouches. They walked off the path and a chill ran up Hugh's arm. He was never usually scared of the darkness. It didn't bother him. But something was different. They bent down to fill the pouches. Mama filled one and handed it to Hugh. She continued to fill each pouch. Hugh could hear something coming. He didn't want to look up. A hand touched his shoulder, and he jumped and went to hit whatever touched him. When he turned, he saw it was only Alwind but he looked worried. He put his finger to his lips to warn them not to say a word. Out of the shadows Hugh could see something coming toward them. It was not like the shadow people. It was bigger but crawled. It was one of the many!! If they made it to the narrow path the creature might not see them. Mama gathered Hugh and covered him. She motioned him to walk carefully but swiftly. She pointed at the sticks and shook her finger to show him he needed to not step on anything that could make noise and bring attention to their way.

Mama knew the light would peek through the darkness any moment. They must hurry. They had almost reached the path when Hugh saw a rock he wanted to jump over. Hugh jumped but hit the corner of the big rock and tripped just as he reached the path. He looked at Mama terrified. Why hadn't he just listened! Why did he not listen more carefully, he thought to himself.

She just picked him up and kissed his head. She looked to Alwind as if to say sorry. But Alwind knew Hugh had made a mistake and did not mean to bring attention to them. There was nothing they could do but hope the creature had not heard them. Mama took Hugh to the rest of the family while Alwind stayed to look out toward the brook to see if the creature had followed them. Mama gathered the family and told them they must hurry on their journey, and they must be silent as they walk. They started packing their bags and pulling their hoods over their heads. The light was just starting to shimmer through the clouds, but it was too late.

Alwind's eye widened as he saw the beast coming towards them. The creature looked quite beautiful. But Alwind knew inside it was nothing but darkness and evil. It gracefully walked towards Alwind. It swayed. Dark green eyes with dark black hair that looked like a horse's beautiful mane. It had the body of a horse, but the skin glistened from the scales that interlocked up and down it's body like chainmail armor. It's face, almost human but the cheekbones were high and sunken in. There were wings that arched back. Its voice was deep.

"Alwind…. we finally found you."

"Be gone Creature, go back to your Wizard. I'm sure you will give him the news you saw me. You cannot cross the light of the path. Leave us alone."

"For now, Alwind…but we are coming! And now that we have found you, the Wizard will be on his way. Be ready Alwind. We are not like the one you serve. There will be no mercy. The Wizard will have them. He will not stop till he has them. The middle child is drawing close to our side. You will see. Run Alwind. We are coming," the beast retorted and shrieked with laughter. She opened her mouth and darkness came pouring out till the creature was no more.

Alwind ran toward his favorite family of seven. The time was now. He didn't have time to form a plan. He silently pleaded to the One who could save them: "Help me please! I cannot do this without you! Help us. We need courage and wisdom. You say I just need to ask and it will be given. I am asking for help. Only you can only save them."

Peace filled his heart with determination. He must do everything he can to get these children to the Armor Giver, and he knew he would have the help he needed. No matter the cost. Alwind pulled Mama and Papa aside and spoke to them quickly and then hugged them both. He called the children.

"Children you must listen. This next part of the journey will be so very hard. But you must trust your Mama and Papa and listen to them. You will be tired but must keep going. You will be hungry, but you must keep going. There is not much time. The Wizard sent out spies. One found us when we went to fill the water pouches. It is no one's fault but we must be off...."

"Alwind I'm so sorry I didn't listen well. This is my fault..." Hugh interrupted.

"Hugh, the point is that from now on you must listen completely, ok? We know you didn't mean to. I forgive you sweet boy. Now let's focus on what to do now ok?" Alwind said, trying to reassure Hugh. Sean frowned at his brother. He wasn't so sure he could let it go as quickly.

"Let's go!" Alwind exclaimed.

They started running on the path. The light was shining which gave them some hope that maybe they could reach the *Mountains of the Cedar Doors* before the Wizard overtook them.

But as they began to go down into the valley of the golden threads, for the valley looked golden as the sunlight hit the wheat stalks, they heard terrifying noises coming from behind them. Alwind threw off his hood and so did Mama and Papa. Sean, Kayleigh and Hugh for the first time could see something glowing from their heads. It was the crown of symbols that Sean had noticed before. They began to each say ancient words together. But the children couldn't hear them clearly as they all were running. Suddenly Alwind stopped. His crown was so bright. The children could hardly see his eyes. He shouted to Mama and Papa:

"I will hold them off. Take them as far as you can and then you know what must happen. Be quick my favorite family of seven. I will miss sharing stories with you. Now run! Till we meet again. And I promise we will. Sean, remember our talk and Hugh, remember my words. Kayleigh, keep helping your Mama and Papa. Be strong. Till then!" Alwind did what he told the children never to do. His body stepped off the path and stood his ground saying the ancient words loudly.

Mama and Papa scooped up Fiona and Liam and told the older three to run. "

"Till then Alwind! Till then dear friend." Shouted Papa.

Alwind smiled and turned to face the darkness. Shrieks of terror came out from the darkness. The creature Hugh had seen was leading the way with another. The Wizard. He was taller than mountains he had seen. His body looked hard as stone, his eyes were completely black and his hair black as night and long. He floated with ease while *the many* seemed to struggle to keep up with him. The Wizard looked less harmless than the creature Hugh thought. He then remembered Alwind's words and focused on running.

Alwind stood still and words flowed out as he touched the crown glowing from his head. As Sean ran, he turned to look. Alwind seemed covered in silvery armor with a sword that seemed to glow. But Alwind did not move forward. He was still holding his sword up high. As the darkness pushed around him a bright light burst from where Alwind was. Sean was too scared to look again. But peeked once more and saw the darkness had been pushed back. Yet, Alwind was not there. Sean looked at Mama and Papa and saw tears falling as they were running. Mama's crown was also still glowing. Sean would ask later what it meant. They kept running for what seemed like an hour. They came near a water brook just before the path up the mountain of the cedar trees began. Papa said they could stop to drink water. They lifted their hoods back over their heads. Mama and Papa looked so tired. They took off their shoes and Hugh gasped as he saw the blisters and open sores that clustered on their feet. Kayleigh opened her pack and opened a jar of aloe and balm she had made. Without a word she went to her Papa and Mama and put the salve on their wounds. Papa and Mama gave her a big hug and kiss. She then put some on her brother's feet and hers. No one spoke. They were too tired. Mama passed out some bread and dried

The Amor Giver

fruits and they ate quietly. Only the sounds of their heavy breathing filled the air. Fiona and Liam climbed on Papa's lap and fell asleep.

Kayleigh quietly asked, "Mama, what happened to Alwind? Will we see him ever again?"

"Alwind fought to protect us. He stood his ground against the Wizard and his many. The Armor Giver gave Alwind a gift to use against the Wizard; it took everything Alwind had to push him back that far. He gave us more time to get to the Armor Giver. You older three are old enough now to be given a gift from the Armor Giver if you choose to take it. But we must get you there. We cannot protect you any longer. The Wizard is coming after all who choose to stay on the narrow path and live outside his shadows. They stay together so we can see when they are coming, but you children do not have that gift yet. You can be tricked loves. For the Wizard can shift and change into figures that seem safe and wonderful. That is why we have taught you the ancient words because the Wizard hates these words. You will know who is true and what is not when you say the words we have taught you. If the figure cries out or covers their ears you will know they are not true to the Armor Giver. They are true to the Wizard and...."

"Wait! What do you mean we must choose? We of course choose against the Wizard, Mama! I'll fight him just like Alwind and send that Wizard army across the world!" Hugh shouted.

"With what Hugh will you fight him with? You are the one who tripped and let them know where we were. And didn't you see? The Wizard was only pushed back and Alwind disappeared. I saw! We have no power against him!"

"Mama, why is the Armor Giver letting good people like Alwind go! Did Alwind die? Did the Wizard capture him? Why doesn't the Armor Giver just come and save us? I don't understand?" Sean said with tears of anger streaming down his face.

Mama hugged Sean and Papa looked at him and said, "Sean boy, firstly, Hugh was forgiven already. He did not mean to alert the creature. You must be forgiving. And Hugh has learned his lesson. He ran as fast as he could this time. Secondly, the Armor Giver will come but not until every land has heard of him and chosen a side. Alwind has gone on son, that is true. We will not see him here again till the Armor Giver comes back to the final battle. He is giving time for people to choose him or the Wizard. He will not force his way on anyone. But he gives a gift to each of us who choose him. The Armor of protection; that will fight against the darkness. Your mother and I have this gift just as Alwind did. This armor will not prolong your life children, only the Armor Giver knows when it is our time. But while you are here it will protect you from the Wizard and his schemes and will shine a light on the darkness he tries to spread. It will keep you on the path of truth. Will you choose it too children? Sean, Kayleigh and Hugh; you are old enough to choose which life you desire. Life in the shadowlands or life filled with light and peace. Which will you choose when you see the Armor Giver? Please choose what we have taught you. If you do, you will see Alwind again and everyone you have loved who has lived on the side of the Armor Giver like Mana and Bapa and Nona and Papa. They went when you were all so small, but they passed on to Mama and me the ancient words. Death lasts for a second loves. But when we go, our second life begins, and it will last forever. Forever is a long time, loves. Forever with the Armor Giver and his light and peace or forever with the Wizard and his many. Take heart children. We will get through this."

The children nodded and cried for Alwind.

Sean asked "Did it hurt him, Mama? Was he scared?"

"Oh son, dying is never easy. But it is not the end. Remember it is not the end love."

"The Ancient words say:
O Death you thought your sting was greater
The Wizard thinks he wins
By taking away the people of light
But he does not know the secret rite
The end is not the end
For He will return again
With those who choose his side.
The Wizard and his many
Will be banished to the depths
For the reign of the Armor Giver
Will go on and never end"

Kayleigh and Sean took comfort in those words. Hugh was very angry that Alwind died. He was furious at himself and at the Wizard but there was also an anger growing toward the Armor Giver. He was confused. Maybe he didn't want to choose any side he thought to himself. He kicked a few rocks and looked out. Mama and Papa told the older kids to huddle next to them on the path. They would get a few hours' rest and then start again they explained. For dear Alwind gave them more time, but the darkness was gaining power and soon the Wizard and his many would return. The children nodded and huddled close together. Hugh let out a sigh and faced the rest. He wasn't going to let anyone see the sadness and regret he felt. The Family of Seven slept fitfully for a few hours. Mama was glad she packed the cotton for their ears so they could soften the shrieks that filled the night.

The darkness was coming again. They were going to have to run again soon. Papa woke first. He lifted his hand to touch Mama's face. She opened her eyes and quickly sat up. She and Papa could feel an urging to get up and go. They wasted no time and woke the rest of the children.

"Mama is it time to eat again?" Liam said as he yawned and opened one sleepy eye.

Everyone laughed. Liam was always ready to eat. Mama pulled out some dates and handed them out. Fiona sang and danced and twirled her hair with her finger as she ate her dates. Sweet Fiona and Liam. They brought the Family of Seven some laughter in the midst of a very hard time.

The family of seven walked for hours and the sun left quickly, covered by clouds to make their surroundings very grey and bleak. They kept following Papa as he held Liam and Fiona. Mama put cotton in their ears to help soften the deafening shrieks of the night.

The mountain path was going to be harder on them. Thankfully the path was lined with trees along it. Mama and Papa kept their hoods down and walked with the little ones. Mama kept Kayleigh with her and was talking to her about herbs and berries and reminding her the differences between the wheat and weeds that grew together. Kayleigh always enjoyed hearing about the different plants, the foods they could make, and the medicines they could make as well. She would sketch pictures of the plants and write down notes in her little book with paper. Kayleigh was quiet and shy and rarely spoke. She was often like a little mama to the babies. They loved to hold her hand and always cried to her when they fell if Mama was away. Kayleigh paid extra attention as Mama spoke to her. She could tell Mama wanted her to remember everything she was saying. After a while they sang Alwind's Song and Papa went through the song with them.

"Children this song is the key to finding the Armor Giver."

The children's eyes grew wide. Papa told them the song was a map. They were headed to the Mountain of Cedars where the children would be tested to follow the right path.

"The door that is opened must be knocked on, but it will not be opened unless your heart is right children. Your heart must be ready to find the Armor Giver. Only then will it open. Next children, you must follow this path all the way to the tree that has the ancient words inscribed. You must remember Alwind's stories and the symbols on his staff. Do you remember children? There will be trees with other symbols. You must go to the tree that matches Alwind's staff. The tree will open to you if you say the ancient words. You each will say the ancient words. The words your heart is drawn to will be the one for you. Do not copy each other. It will not work. If you choose the Armor Giver, say the ancient words we have taught you. Let's sing the song again children."

The children grew worried. Would they remember all the words Mama and Papa taught them? Wouldn't they be there anyways to help them along?

"Papa are we to be there alone?" Kayleigh asked timidly.

"I don't know love. Mama and I want to be there but there will come a point where you must go alone and receive the gift from the Armor Giver. It will be all right whether we are there or not there. Don't worry about that now. Come on, I know what will cheer us up. Fiona girl, come sing us a song and bring us some sunshine, huh?" asked Papa.

Fiona opened her mouth without any extra prompting and sang loudly,

"The Armor Giver loves us so
So, I will sing with joy and know
The light will come and the dark
will go. The Armor Giver
loves us so!"

Everyone smiled and joined Fiona. Liam started dancing and making silly faces. As they hiked up the hill the Family of Seven didn't notice that their legs were so tired anymore. They marched together bravely. Sean and Hugh lagged a bit behind. Sean was still upset about Hugh falling and alerting the Wizard's many, and Hugh was upset with himself as well. Often times when Hugh was upset with himself, he often took it out on his older brother by teasing him a bit. Hugh bumped into his brother to see if Sean would smile at him, but Sean ignored him. Hugh bumped him again and this got Sean even angrier, so he shoved Hugh down hard. Hugh looked up with tears in his eyes. Sean regretted it immediately. He stuck out his hand and Hugh looked away. As he looked back, he saw the darkness coming quickly. He got up and pushed Sean's hand away but told him to hurry up with him. Sean looked back in fear and ran quickly to catch up with Hugh and the rest. They shouted to their Mama and Papa. Mama and Papa's crown began to glow brighter. They turned back and saw. There was no escaping. The Wizard was coming. Deep darkness was taking over the grey clouds. They knew it was time. Mama and Papa looked at their children and then looked at each other and nodded.

Mama turned and said, "There is not much time. We will give you enough time to get to the doors. You must hurry. Do not stop. Keep to the path children. If you must sleep, you must only go onto the trees that are on the path. The Wizard will not touch those trees. Kayleigh, you know what you've been learning, you must do your best with food and medicine love. Sean, you are in charge, but a good leader listens too and encourages. Remember that love. Forgive and move on. Hugh, you must listen to Sean and Kayleigh but stand for what is true. You are so smart and brave. Be strong children. We love you always and forever. Remember the ancient words and stay on the narrow path. Fiona and Liam must stay with us. You must get to the Armor Giver. Follow the narrow path. Remember Alwind's song. It has the answers. Be quick my loves. You will need each other for this. Say the song and ancient words every moment you have children. It will get you to Him. There's not much time. Sean be wise, Kayleigh be brave, Hugh be strong. Run!! Till we meet again loves. Remember to believe and we will meet again'. Now go! Go!!!!!! Keep the Path!!!"

Sean and Kayleigh and Hugh began running. They knew Alwind's fate but would their Mama and Papa and brother and sister have the same fate as Alwind?

The Amor Giver

They ran fast and could hear the shrieks coming towards them. They looked back and saw Mama and Papa holding hands and holding the babies' hands. Such a strange thing was that it looked like the glow was also coming from Liam and Fiona, but how? They stood still just as Alwind did, and they could see their mouths moving. Again, it looked as if they were covered in a shiny covering, metallic-like, just like Alwind. They turned and ran faster up the mountain path. They needed to get to those doors. As they got up the first mountain a huge flash of light surged from where their parents and siblings were. Sean could see a burst of light go high into the sky. The darkness had been pushed back even farther than the last time.

Tears streamed down the siblings faces as they ran and ran. They held hands automatically, as if holding on to each other's hand meant they would be ok. They ran as the darkness settled across the sky. Kayleigh stopped the boys and pointed to a tree that was on the path. She climbed up the thick branches and the boys followed. She pulled out the water pouches and some nuts and dry bread. She told the boys they would have food for a couple days, but she would need to be on the lookout for more plants and food. They ate quietly at first. Hugh burst into tears smacking his hand on his head and calling himself horrible names and crying out that he was sorry. Sean came to the same branch and hugged Hugh and reassured Hugh it was not his fault, but that the Wizard was evil, and it was the Wizard's fault. Sean stayed there with Hugh and hugged his brother till he fell asleep. Sean kept wiping away the tears and wondering what the light that went up into the sky was. It happened differently than Alwind. Why? He pondered this till he too fell asleep. Kayleigh cried quietly and recited the Ancient Words Mama and Papa had taught her. She would only let them rest a couple hours. Light would come again soon. Hugh slept on Sean's shoulder and was thankful for his brother's forgiveness. The family of seven was now a family of three. Kayleigh prayed and hoped they would make it to the Armor Giver together. She couldn't bear losing anyone else.

Chapter 5

Mountain Doors of Cedars

Sunlight peeked through the tree that the family of three were sleeping heavily in. Kayleigh was the first to wake up. No sign of the darkness appeared but she knew she needed to get her brothers up. Time could not be wasted. She looked into her pouch and sighed. There was not much left to eat. Hopefully she could find some seeds or wheat or berries while they walked up the mountain.

"Sean and Hugh, wake up. We need to start walking to get to the Mountain Doors of Cedars. Wake up." she said sweetly. Sean opened one eye and then the other. He smiled at his sister and tried to stretch but something was behind him. He turned and saw Hugh curled up behind him. He shook his brother a little and told him they needed to get up. The three climbed down the tree and looked around very cautiously. Kayleigh handed them the last of Mama's bread and some dates. They each sat for a moment, they didn't want to eat the last of Mama's bread.

Kayleigh took a deep breath, holding back tears and said, "Let's give thanks brothers. Mama's last words to us was to keep the ancient words."

With that the three sang somberly:
"Oh, Giver of daily bread
Oh, Giver of Life
For this day we thank you
For what is ahead we give to you
Thank you for another day
Thank you for our family
Oh, Giver we are truly Thankful to you."

They ate silently. Hugh had tears streaming down his face, but he made no noise. He turned his back to them and looked up at the mountain. Thinking of Alwind's tale, he wondered what waited for them at the Mountain Doors of Cedars. They had climbed up two mountain peaks and saw at least three more. But so far, no doors to be seen. They had a long journey ahead. He'd go fill up the water pouches.

"I'm going to fill up the water pouches. I have to go off the path but it's close. It's the only way."

"I'll go with you. We shouldn't separate. Kayleigh, you stay on the path, though, and watch us." Sean said matter-of-factly.

Hugh just nodded and frowned. He wanted to be alone. He wanted to find the creature and hurt it. He wanted to be found. He kicked some stones as they walked. Sean gave Hugh some space. They got to the water brook and started filling the water pouches. Sean was happy to have the extra ones as it would save them time from stopping. A rustle in the brushes by the trees startled them. Hugh frowned and got up. Sean went to grab his arm, but he couldn't let go of the water pouches. Hugh lunged for the noise and went looking for what was making the noise. He was ready to fight whatever was coming their way. Sean didn't know whether to yell for Hugh or run after him. He just quietly whispered the ancient words his Papa had taught him.

"Ask and it will be given
Seek and you shall find
For the One who is good
Will provide all you need
There is no need to fear
You must just believe
Call on Him and He will help"

Hugh was farther than Sean could see. Where was he?

Hugh burst out in anger "Where are you!?! Is that you, creature? Are you spying on us for the Wizard? I'm not afraid of you and your stupid Wizard!!!!" I hate you for what you did!!!! Come out!"

"I'm sorry to say that you will not be fighting anyone today. I am a creature. But I am no friend of the Wizard. I do need help. Would you mind helping me young man? I am over here in the blackberry bush to your right. I've seemed to have tangled myself in the thorns of the blackberries. Would you mind untangling me?" asked the creature.

Hugh didn't know if he could trust the voice, he was hearing but he was not afraid. He turned to his right and peered into the blackberry bushes. He stepped back in disbelief. Was that a raven talking to him? Was he hearing right? He stepped forward again and could see the left wing of the raven was indeed tangled. He carefully lifted the wing away from the thorns and then picked the raven out of the bush and put it on the ground. For a moment the bird stretched out its wings and hopped around. Hugh scratched his head and was about to walk away when the raven began to speak again.

"Thank you, kind boy. I thought for a moment I might be stuck there till I got eaten by a shadow person or by that nasty creature that serves the Wizard. I suppose that is who you were talking about. I'm Ravenbird. What is your name?" asked Ravenbird

Hugh's eyes grew wide, and a huge smile spread across his face. "I did hear you!! You can talk to me! How can you talk to me? Oh, my goodness, I can't wait for my sister and brother to meet you. My name is Hugh! We are trying to reach the Mountain Doors of Cedar. Yes, I hate the Creature that serves the Wizard. The Wizard killed my friend Alwind and my parents and baby brother and sister."

"Oh, my boy, I'm so sad to hear this. I would be happy to help you find the Mountain Doors of Cedar. But I'm afraid your brother and sister may not be able to hear me if they are older than you. Most children stop talking to us once they reach a certain age and they often forget we ever talked back to them. But let's go. I am a follower of the Armor Giver. Faithful to him alone. I will do what I can to help." Said Ravenbird. The Ravenbird went to fly but squawked aloud and looked at his left wing.

Hugh bent down to look closely and saw there was a small gash.

"Looks like I will be helping you first Ravenbird. Come on." Hugh gently scooped him up and noticed small specks of white along the crown of the bird's head. It reminded him of something, but he wasn't sure what of.

Hugh ran back through the brush to the brook. A look of relief could be seen across Sean's face which quickly was replaced by irritation.

"Hugh what would have happened if you had been caught. I know you are angry; I am too but you can't just take off like that. You need to start thinking better!"

Hugh rolled his eyes, "I know, ok. But it wasn't what we thought. Look. This raven was caught in some blackberry bushes. Oh, that reminds. Kayleigh!!! Kayleigh, come here! I found blackberries. And I found an injured Raven. He can't fly…he needs…"

Sean interrupted, "You can't be serious! We don't have time for this Hugh. Mama and Papa gave us a task and we need to finish it."

"But Sean the bird asked for my help. His name is Ravenbird. He says he is on the side of the Armor Giver and will help us. Go on Ravenbird, introduce yourself." Hugh said pleadingly to Ravenbird.

Kayleigh and Sean looked quickly at one another with concern in their eyes and on their faces.

It did look like Ravenbird might speak as it opened its mouth but all they heard was squawking. Hugh was watching his brother and sister and could see right away they didn't hear anything. Wow! He had a friend that only he could talk to. He smirked and decided to just focus on Ravenbird's injury.

"All he is doing is squawking Hugh." Sean said.

"Well anyways, Kayleigh, look at his wing. You were always so good with the animals at home. Do you have anything to put on his cut?"

Kayleigh took Ravenbird from Hugh and took the aloe balm she had. She gently put balm on the cut.

"Ahh thank you kind girl. That feels so much better. Hugh, tell her I said thank you."

"Ugh, Ravenbird says thank you Kayleigh." He said hesitantly.

Kayleigh laughed a bit. "Well Hugh, I don't know what to make of this but Sean, we need to keep this raven with us. Mama and Papa would have wanted us to care for him. You know that. It doesn't matter how Hugh found him. But Hugh, please remember what Mama and Papa said. We must do everything together. We need each other."

Hugh shook his head in agreement. Sean scratched his head and sighed. "Ok. Let's go pick those berries and then we need to start up the mountain. The doors must be at one of these mountains. I've counted at least three peaks. But there could be more.... mmmmm! Did you taste these? That raven at least brought us some food. I'm glad you found him Hugh."

The children picked all the berries and then headed up the mountain on the path. It was hot. It would be a hard day's climb. But they each felt a bit of relief to have the raven with them. They didn't know why but for some reason they didn't feel so alone. They walked even when the sun went away. Kayleigh, like her mom, let some of the berries fall off the path every once in a while. She left them for the shadow people who were lost. They often said aloud Alwind's Tale and took turns sharing the ancient words. When one would stumble over the words they would help one another. Hugh had the hardest time. Sean would grow impatient at times and finish it for him while Kayleigh would give clues to Hugh. Hugh silently wasn't sure he wanted to meet the Armor Giver. Why didn't he save their parents? Why didn't he save Liam and Fiona? They were so little. Did they suffer? The thought of that brought out an anger in him that he couldn't explain. He'd beat that Wizard and that creature one day. He would.

"Hugh, I can sense something is wrong. You are angry right?" Ravenbird asked as they walked.

Hugh sniffed and walked a little ahead Kayleigh and Sean so he could talk to Ravenbird. He answered quietly,

"I am having a hard time yes. I want to kill the Wizard and his creature and I'm not so sure I want to meet the Armor Giver anymore. I know Mama and Papa told me it was the only way for me to see them again but Ravenbird, why didn't he save them? Why?"

"I don't know boy. But I agree with your Mama and Papa. They must have been so brave to stay loyal and trust the Armor Giver. Don't forget Hugh, the ancient words:

The Wizard and his many will rise
They will claim to have victory
But in their pride
They will stumble and fall
Beneath the weight
Of their great mistake
They thought they made the
Armor Giver disappear

But on that day, He will reappear
And with him an army so great
That the Wizard will quake
And be beaten by the Light
That will wipe out the darkness
And set all things right.

"I remember Papa telling us this. Thank you. I feel better for some reason. I have no answers, but I feel better. Thank you, Ravenbird."

"This is our hope too boy. We are waiting. All that has been created, we wait. We endure and suffer from the Wizard's darkness and the people of the shadows. They walk around us confused, scared and often desperate for relief. They try everything and anything. It's horrible. So many of my friends snatched and eaten without any satisfaction from them. Their bellies remain hungry." Ravenbird said sadly.

Sean interrupted them. "Let's climb up this tree. I think we need to rest. I was hoping we'd see the doors, but they aren't here yet. I wonder how we will know which door to go through?"

"Remember," Kayleigh said,
Seek the truth
And you will find
Which door to take
Which is right
With just a knock
It will be opened
Only good intentions

Or you'll be forbidden

"What does only good intentions mean?" asked Hugh

"It means you might not make it with us brother." teased Sean.

"Haha, very funny." Hugh said flatly.

"I think I remember Alwind's story about the doors. He talked about the Mountain with the Doors of Cedar. I wonder if there are really wooden doors or if it will be like Alwind's house. Remember the Cedar tree carved into the side of the mountain? I wonder...." Kayleigh sat in her thoughts and then handed out the pouches of water to everyone. Everyone was so thirsty. The air was so dry and warm. She passed out the aloe balm to put on their feet and then handed everyone some mint oil to help them feel a little fresher and more relaxed.

She sang them a song and said goodnight. She was exhausted and worried about finding food. She also noticed the water brook was lower than the last time. She hoped they'd at least be able to keep finding water. She drifted off to sleep.

"Hugh, do you really hear Ravenbird speaking. Come on, tell me the truth. Is this one of your tricks again? It just worries me if you are talking to a bird and not really hearing it."

"I can't prove to you I can hear him, ok? I mean you can think I'm crazy, but I can. He reminded me today that even though I don't understand what is going on, I need to trust in the Ancient words. He reminded me that even though I couldn't kill the Wizard and his creature today, that one day they will get what's coming. I hope I'm there. I'm so angry. Don't tell Kayleigh, I don't want to worry her, but I am angry, Sean. And I'm sorry this is all my fault. I never meant for them to find us. I'm so sorry brother..." tears came down Hugh's face again.

"Mama and Papa forgave you Hugh and I....and I do too. I just miss Mama and Papa so much and I feel so scared to be brave. I have to think everything out. I feel so stressed knowing it's my job now to keep us all together and safe. But I'll tell you a secret. I wish I was a bit braver and not scared of anything like you. Come on let's get some rest."

Sean sat with his arm around Hugh and Ravenbird crawled to Sean's lap and laid there looking up at him. Sean could feel it looking at him. "I wonder...." Sean thought to himself. He shook away the thought and yawned really big. He closed his eyes picturing Mama and Papa's faces. Before he could think of anything else his mind finally felt tired, and he drifted off to sleep. Ravenbird smiled and closed his eyes too.

They slept for just a few hours and continued on. The path seemed to go on forever. They were thankful when trees would appear. They also were thankful they could find water near the path. However, as two days went by Kayleigh was starting to get worried as no berries or seeds or even plants could be found. She started giving them less berries when they rested, and she ran out of the dates and nuts Mama had given to her. She was trying not to panic but Mama told her this was her job - to find the food, to make the medicines. But how? How could she if there was nothing growing?

"We need to refill the pouches brothers. I'm so worried. There is nothing growing around here. How am I going to make us anything or pick anything when there's nothing to pick? How about you two go refill the pouches quickly. We've reached a flat part. I hope this lasts longer than the last three mountains. I will hold Ravenbird."

The boys went off the path and quickly found the water brook. While they filled the pouches, Kayleigh put Ravenbird down to let him walk a bit and sat down on a big rock by the path. Kayleigh sighed and said, "I wish you could talk to me Ravenbird. I am having such a hard day. I'm so scared we won't find any food. I can't let Mama and Papa down and let us all die of hunger while searching for these doors! What am I going to do?" A tear fell down her face.

Ravenbird looked at her and then stretched out his wings. "Oh, your wing looks all better. Do you feel better Raven?"

Ravenbird flapped his wings and to his surprise he was able to fly again. Kayleigh smiled as she watched him glide around her. Her smile though turned to panic as she watched Ravenbird fly away. "No! Come back! Hugh will be so upset with me! Please!"

Hugh saw Ravenbird flying away as Sean and him ran back.

"Ravenbird! You said you would help us! Why are you leaving! Don't leave!!!! How can you leave! How can you go!" Hugh screamed. He ran toward the bird, but Sean grabbed him as Hugh had almost run right off the mountain side. Hugh and Sean wrestled for a moment. Hugh pushed Sean away. Sean yelled "Enough!! I've had enough! Hugh that was just a dumb bird and you lied to us! You just made up a game and you need to stop! Good for the bird. It's better. Birds are supposed to fly! Not talk to humans. Now stop being stupid and let's go!"

Hugh groaned in anger and started running up the path. He would never trust anything again. Stupid Raven. He made him a fool. Why did he leave them? Why did he say he would help? Hugh ran until he felt his lungs burst.

Sean and Kayleigh ran as well but could not keep up.

"Sean that was too harsh. I know you want him to grow up but he's younger than us. That bird brought him comfort. He is hurting and…"

"And so are we Kayleigh!!" Sean burst out with tears in his eyes. "So are we!"

They both had tears as they ran to Hugh. They nearly bumped into him as they hadn't noticed he had stopped and was looking down at the ground. There at his feet was Ravenbird. It had around it a cloth full of wheat, another small cloth of seeds and nuts, and a cloth of berries.

Sean rubbed his eyes in disbelief. Kayleigh picked up Ravenbird and hugged it.

"Oh, you brilliant little thing! You heard my every word and understood me! You can talk! Oh, Hugh, you were telling the truth! This bird understood us. He knew we needed food. What a smart little raven. You took my little cloths and filled them with food."

"I'm, I'm, I'm… sorry Hugh. I'm so sorry I called you terrible names and didn't believe you. Ravenbird thank you for helping us and for helping my brother. Thank you." Cried out Sean.

Hugh stood there and, in an instant, this little angry child felt such happiness. His anger melted away and he took Ravenbird and hugged him.

"You kept your promise. I'm sorry I doubted you. Thank you for coming back, Ravenbird." Hugh said happily.

"I told you I am faithful to the Armor Giver, and I am also a faithful friend. As your friend Hugh, I must caution you to let the anger you feel go. It will not bring your Mama and Papa back and it will get in the way of what they want for you. Don't let the Wizard fool you with his way of feeling things. Those dark feelings come from him. He wants you to feel darkness, to feel hopelessness, to feel anger. That is not our way. That should not be yours. Keep fighting against it. I'll be here to help." Hugh shook his head meekly and kept petting Ravenbird as he thought about those words.

Kayleigh started a fire with the sharp rocks of the mountain and used a salt stone and water and the wheat heads to prepare bread. She grinded the wheat and then added flour and salt she grinded from the salt stone. She baked the bread in the fire and then quickly put the fire out so the spies of the Wizard would not see the smoke. Well, she hoped at least they hadn't. But she saw the darkness coming. It was making up speed and it was travelling faster than before.

They didn't realize how hungry they were. The bread tasted so good. It quickly disappeared. They finished and then began walking again. The path seemed to narrow a bit and it was harder to stay completely on it. But there was no place for shadows on the path, which kept them safe from the shadow people and the Wizard and his many. They could not walk on the narrow path. Nothing that had chosen the Wizard's side could walk it. For the ancient words say:

The narrow path will be walked by those
Who choose what is right and it will expose
Those who choose to walk the wide lands
They are the ones with evil in hand
But those who walk the narrow road
Will always have light for their feet to go
Till the Armor Giver's land, you approach
Though it's not easy, you will always find hope
Stay on the narrow path
Away from the Wizard's snatch

But that left them without shade. The little forests in the mountains were becoming fewer and fewer. It left them quite hot and thirsty as they walked. For the sun seemed to no longer be a friendly welcome. Instead, its heat and dry air left them miserable and tired as if the Wizard had managed to corrupt the sun itself. Yet the children knew misery is what the Wizard always produced. After what seemed like hours, they stopped mid-way up the mountain side to drink more water and eat some bread and blackberries.

Kayleigh handed out the food while Sean handed out the pouches of water. They quickly drank all their water and desperately wanted more. But there was nothing near them right now. They knew it would be a while.

"Ravenbird, can you fly ahead of us to see if there is water nearby?" asked Hugh.

"Of course, just make sure you all stay directly on the path. I feel something is close by. Not quite human, not my kind either. Stay on the path and remember how to tell what side one is on. Say the Ancient words and if they join, you will know."

"Ok" Hugh said, as he half listened, and half played with a stick he had found. It snapped and he tossed away, sighing with boredom. Off Ravenbird went. He would go as fast as he could to find water as he wasn't too sure his little friend had paid enough attention.

Hugh told the others where Ravenbird was going and what he said about the path; forgetting to mention Ravenbird felt something was close by. They nodded and hoped Ravenbird would let them know soon if they were close to the top of the mountain and if there was water close to the path. The sun was warm, and the air was extremely hot. Sean could see Kayleigh and Hugh were having a hard time. He went to each one and took their bags. He would carry them as far as he could. Determination set in and he didn't complain or slow down. He would keep his word to Papa.

Once they reached the top of the mountain, they lay down on the path. They were so happy to reach a stretch of flat pathway. They noticed to the side there was an opening in the rocks, like a small cave. They wondered if it was the cave they were supposed to go through, but it didn't seem right that it would be away from the path. The sunlight was fading, and they all could hear each other breathing. Suddenly they heard a noise, and they sat up instantly. Sean told Kayleigh and Hugh to get behind him. The sound seemed to be coming from the shrubs by the cave.

"Ravenbird, is that you?" Hugh asked.

"Who is Ravenbird?" came a response from the shrubs.

"Who are you? Come out so we can see you." Sean stated.

The figure came closer and closer. It was a beautiful cat with green, emerald eyes and its coat was a dark black. It had tiny speckles of white on the crown of its head too like Ravenbird. As it came toward them it stopped in front of them and looked them in the eyes.

"Hello children. I am Truecrea. I am a friend of all. What are you doing up in these mountains? You look so tired and thirsty. Come with me and I can show you where the water is. I also know where to find some delicious food. Once you taste it, you will want more and more. Come follow me." She said invitingly and turned to walk toward the cave.

Hugh looked at his sister and brother. They seemed to have understood for their eyes and mouths were wide open in shock. Why could they understand this cat but not Ravenbird and where was Ravenbird. Hugh looked around and tried to see if he could see Ravenbird in the distance.

"Who are you looking for boy? You seemed to be looking for someone or something?"

Sean realized he wasn't hearing things and decided to speak up for Hugh. He could see Hugh didn't trust this cat by the frown on his face, but they were so thirsty, they really needed water. Maybe this cat was a friend. They were supposed to go through a cave. But he didn't see the door.

"My brother is just looking for his pet bird. It flew away. Now you said you knew where there is water. Why isn't there any close to the path? There is always water from the flat parts of the path.

"Silly child. There is not shade here or even any trees. Don't you see the water needed to be kept safe up here. That is why the one who makes things puts it in the cave. Now come and I will show you the way."

"But how are we understanding you?" Hugh asked.

"Oh, we animals can speak; most people never take the time to believe or to listen. I can help you children. I can take you to safety. Come, let's go."

"Sean, we need to wait for Ravenbird. He said he would help us. He went to look for water. He will come back…."

"Yeah, but if the water is in the cave he might be flying forever before he finds water. There's water right here. The cat seems friendly. I don't know. It is off the path, but we are so thirsty. Kayleigh what do you think?"

Kayleigh was mesmerized by the beauty of the cat. She smiled and the cat came close to the path and let her pet her. Kayleigh loved animals. She happily helped Mama and Papa with their animals, nursing them when they were sick, petting them and giving them extra love. Animals would often allow Kayleigh to pet them before the other children. Kayleigh just loved looking at this cat. It's a shiny perfect coat of black and her beautiful deep green eyes. Her eyes were almost hypnotizing Kayleigh thought to herself. She secretly had wanted Ravenbird to talk to her making her a little jealous, but she would never admit that. All animals usually chose her first, she took pride in that. Perhaps that's why she trusted Truecrea immediately as she came to her first.

"She seems so sweet and what an amazing thing that we can all understand her. She must be good like Ravenbird. But maybe we should walk a bit further. Truecrea are there other entrances to the cave in the mountains? Can we walk a bit further?"

"Yes, I can take you when you are ready. I will walk with you."

So, the three kept on the path and the cat followed beside them. The cat would stay close to the path near Kayleigh asking for more cuddles here and there. Kayleigh would stop and bend over to pet her. Sean suggested they practice the Ancient words, but the cat kept interrupting them with stories of the mountain. The cat also seemed very interested in their family, asking them questions. Kayleigh shared about their journey and how she missed her Mama and Papa. Sean grew a bit worried as he wasn't so sure they should be telling everything to a creature they didn't really know. And he was getting quite frustrated because the cat would not stop taking Kayleigh's attention. They needed to remember the Ancient words. They would forget if they didn't practice.

Hugh kept turning back to see if he could see Ravenbird. He didn't know why but he didn't like this cat. He frowned and sighed loudly every time they stopped for Kayleigh to pet the stupid cat. He also noticed the cat didn't walk directly on the path but just close enough to talk to them or receive a pet from Kayleigh.

They walked for maybe an hour or two but when they stopped everything looked as it did when they first began and to their left again was an opening to what seemed to be a cave.

"Are you ready to drink water and eat good food children? After you can take the inside path and get to where you want to go in the shade and coolness of the cave." asked Truecrea.

"Thank you Truecrea. You are so helpful. Brothers, I think we should go. What if this was the cave the ancient words spoke of. Maybe this is it…"

"Kayleigh, the Mountain Doors of Cedar would have a door or at least a cedar carving like Alwind's. This isn't it…."

"Why silly boy this is the Mountain Doors of Cedar. How old do you think the caves are? Time has weathered the doors, that is all. Now come, let's get you some water"

"But it's not on the path…" interrupted Hugh. "Mama and Papa said the path would take us…"

"But it did children. You are just tired and too weak to see it. Look, can't you see the pieces of wood hanging from the cave."

The children looked and they blinked a few times because they suddenly saw wood clearly where they stood hanging partly on the cave opening. Maybe Truecrea was right. Maybe the path only took them so far. And the door was there, they were just too tired to see. Yes, they were just too tired to see. Kayleigh thought to herself. She motioned to her brothers that they should follow Truecrea. Sean seemed convinced as well. He trusted Kayleigh and she seemed so sure. Hugh on the other hand shrugged his shoulders and said, "whatever."

"That's it, children, yes you see now don't you. Come Kayleigh, you come first. Kayleigh stepped one foot off the path and the cat affectionately rubbed around her leg. Kayleigh smiled and turned to take Sean and Hugh's hand to have them follow. The boys took one foot off the path when suddenly Hugh felt something pulling his shirt back. He turned and saw Ravenbird.

"Get them back on the path Hugh!! That is not a friend! You must show them! Say the Ancient words." The cat meowed angrily at the Ravenbird.

"Get back on the path Kayleigh and Sean!" yelled Hugh as he stepped back and yanked their hands to get their attention.

"Friend or foe
We will know
For on the path
Friend can go
But if they don't
Then you must beware
For they belong to the
Wizard's snare"

The cat began to scream and cover its ears.

Kayleigh froze in fear. Sean tried pulling her back onto the path. She let go and covered her mouth in horror as the cat kept screaming. She stumbled forward completely off the path.

"Kayleigh come on!! Get on the path!"

Just as she turned to step back, the cat growled, and fangs shot out from its mouth began to laugh. That laugh! Hugh knew that terrible laugh.

"Creature!" Hugh yelled. Anger arose and he and Sean bolted off the path to grab their sister. They both grabbed Kayleigh but before they got to the path Creature struck Hugh on the leg with a painful bite. And scratched Sean's leg with its sharp claws causing him to cry out in pain.

They jumped onto the path and Ravenbird flew at Creature pecking it's face when it could.

"Get away Creature, go to your master. You can't have them now!" Ravenbird yelled at it.

Creature morphed into its being and snarled,

"You foolish bird, I should have known they had help. It doesn't matter, the boys won't last the night, especially without water or food. Hahaha!!!! The Wizard is coming! He is coming!" and it opened its mouth and darkness again poured out as it disappeared into the darkness.

"I'm so sorry brothers, I'm so sorry! I wasn't paying close enough attention. Ugh...I just saw a beautiful cat and I was jealous Hugh could hear Ravenbird and I couldn't when I love animals so much. Ugh!!!!! What is wrong with me!" Kayleigh groaned and wrung her hands tightly and then quickly she reached into her bag.

"Ravenbird, I cannot understand you, but I must find water, I must clean their wounds. Please help me, please. Did you find water? She desperately asked.

Ravenbird seemed to shake his head yes. He flew to the ground and picked up what he had flown back with. He came with a pouch full of water and also a pouch with some herbs he had picked. Kayleigh's eyes widened and thankfulness filled her heart.

"Oh Ravenbird, you brilliant friend. How did you know I would need these?"

She took the water and poured it on Sean's gash. It was deep. She would need to close it. Hugh's bite was just on the surface of his skin thankfully. She cleaned it and put a mix of lavender and juniper leaf paste onto the bite. She had Hugh take some water.

She then cleaned Sean's wound and filled the gash with the lavender and juniper paste and then made a paste of wheat flour and water and covered the gash with it. She would need to do this twice a day. She hoped they could find water and more wheat. She had Sean finish the water. She was so thirsty. She turned and found Ravenbird had brought more water in a pouch.

"Thank you so much. I was so thirsty. Can I go with you to get the water Ravenbird?" Ravenbird seemed to shake his head no and went over to cuddle with Hugh. Hugh stroked his head.

"Thank you for saving my family, again." Hugh smiled down at his friend Ravenbird.

"You must stay on the path Hugh. The path to the Armor Giver will not be confusing. It is straight and will not lead you to the shadows. You three must practice Alwind's tale and the ancient words more, or you will be tricked again. Please, you are tired but have them practice the tale."

"Sean and Kayleigh, I know we are tired but let's honor Mama and Papa. We almost forgot all they taught us. We need to practice the ancient words much more tomorrow but let's end the day with Alwind's tale. We can just lean against these rocks on the path and sleep. It will be safe."

They all agreed. They leaned against the rocks and the family of three could be heard singing Alwind's Tale till they drifted off to sleep. Ravenbird cuddled up to Hugh but did not shut his eyes.

The next morning, they found more wheat and berries by their feet and each of their pouches filled with water. Ravenbird must have worked all night. They all stroked his back and thanked him. Kayleigh cleaned Sean's wound and packed it again. It was healing well thankfully and quicker than she thought. She quietly thanked the Armor Giver as that cut had been so deep. Yet she didn't need as much paste this time. Hugh's leg also looked better as she put more aloe balm on it. Everyone seemed to feel a little more hopeful this morning.

They continued on the path for a few hours, each taking turns reciting the ancient words. Just as they reached the mountain peak of what seemed like their seventh mountain climb, they stood in awe of what they saw next. This mountain top was surrounded by doors. Each door had carvings and the doors were made of stone, but each door had the cedar tree carved into their stony bodies. There were seven doors. Which one were they supposed to take? They looked the same! They stood there looking up and each were really wishing their Mama and Papa were there at that moment. They would know which door. They would know what to do. They unconsciously grabbed each other's hands. When they did, they felt a strengthening. They each took a deep breath and started to walk forward. Together, they would do this together.

Chapter 6

Just a Knock

Each door had a path. They were all different. Which path? It looked like each went on forever. The doors were huge. They must have been built by giants, the children thought to themselves. Hugh was the first to let go of their hands and scratched his head in wonder.

"Yeah, I don't really want to walk each path and try each door. There has to be a clue in Alwind's song. Kayleigh, can you sing it again?"

"Sure." Kayleigh said.

"Above the clouds
Above our lands
Above the dark and evil hands
Hear my child in this song
The secret hope that can be found
Follow down
The narrow path
Run my child
Do not look back
The shield of light
It will protect you
Run my child
Run to the mountain
To the Doors of Cedars

Seek the truth
And you will find
Which door to take
Which is right
With just a knock
It will be opened
Only good intentions
Or you'll be forbidden

Look for the ancient words
Inscribed on the Ancient tree
From birth you will have
known them

Read them right for
They must be spoken
If you are worthy
The gift will be given
Beware of yourself
use only when right
Or it will be taken
For it holds the secret light
That will send away
The Wizard and his many
And reveal what is hidden
Hush my child
You must Listen
Hush my child
You must Listen
Follow the whisper
Watch out for the Wizard
Follow the whisper
And help will come
from the Armor Giver
Yes, help will come
From the Armor Giver..........

"Ok, so we are at the doors. We are seeking the truth, but which path leads to the right place? I mean they're all different. Sean, which way do we go? Which one should we try?"

Sean walked forward and stared at each path. He looked back. The darkness seemed to be gaining speed. Or maybe it was just his eyes, but he knew they didn't have time to check each path. They needed to choose right. He closed his eyes, trying to imagine Papa. His Papa, so strong and tall and yet always ready to answer Sean's questions. He could picture Papa so clearly. He didn't want to open his eyes.

"Papa, what do we do? Armor Giver help us."

"Straight, follow the straight path." Sean heard a whisper.

"What did you say Kayleigh?" he asked.

"I didn't say anything. Did you hear a voice, Sean?" asked Kayleigh.

Sean nodded. Hugh was distracted looking around at the paths.

Sean tried to listen again. He heard nothing.

Sean thought deeper, trying to picture Papa sharing the Ancient words. What would he say. What would Papa say. He gasped and opened his eyes. It was like he could hear his voice so clearly.

"I know what Papa would have us do! Remember the ancient words:

"Take a firm hold though your hands are tired
 Stand steady, though your legs feel on fire
 Walk on and make a straight path to go
 Then those who are weaker will surely know
 Where to go and they will not fall
 They will only get stronger and stand tall"

"Don't you see?" Sean asked. Kayleigh smiled and nodded. Hugh still looked puzzled.

"We are so tired, but we must keep going. We don't have time to go slow. Look behind us, the Wizard is on his way. The noises at night are getting stronger. But the Ancient words say make a straight path. I will lead us. We must not separate. Hugh, you must listen to me this time. We must hold on to each other. Follow my footsteps, ok?

"But Sean, which door is it? There's seven! How do you know which path and which door?" asked Hugh

"Don't you see? The Armor Give does not make things confusing. It's simple. It's the door in the middle, right in front of us. It's the only straight path. Come on. Ravenbird, I think it's important you stay on my shoulder. We are meant to stay on the path. I have a bad feeling about the other paths. I think they might be filled with traps. Don't fly right now."

They took hold of each other's hands in birth order. Sean first, then Kayleigh and then Hugh. Hugh reluctantly grabbed hold. He should be in the lead. He's braver. But he would keep his promise to Mama and Papa. He wished he could remember the ancient words like Sean could. How did he even remember Papa saying that? And why did the Armor Giver want them all to memorize these stupid ancient words and have to follow them so carefully? Hugh could feel himself feeling restless. He clenched his teeth and gave a big sigh.

"Ugh, just keep walking", he told himself, "Stop trying to think of things to be mad at."

Their path was straight and seemed so simple, so easy. The path seemed to be made of stone but there was nothing growing on it. The children could see two shadow people traveling the other paths. Some paths were crooked and windy with rocks and sand all over the ground, others looked wide, with soft sand and nothing else, and were very spacious and others were narrow but wavy and tall grass filled in the pathway. The children looked around and noticed darkness taking over the lingering light. They kept walking. They also shouted out to the shadow-people to stay off those paths. They told them it was a trap, but they wouldn't listen. They put their arms to their ears or eyes as if the children offended them with every warning. Hugh kept screaming at them to not be stupid and to not follow the wrong paths, but they just kept on going until the Family of Three watched in horror as they spotted one of the shadow people scream out in panic as something grabbed them and they sank into the sand. Hugh almost ran to help them when Sean reminded him, they had to stay on the path. The shadow person didn't listen to them, there was nothing they could do. They turned and saw the other shadow-person on the narrow path with the wavy grass suddenly be grabbed by something as well and disappear into the tall grass. Only maddening shrieks could be heard. Darkness hovered around them at that moment. Kayleigh began to sing Alwind's tale to keep herself from crying.

Sean saw the light stay on their path. He knew for sure they were on the right one. The light settled just in front of their feet. Just enough to see what was right in front of them. With more determination than ever he ran onward clutching tightly and focused on only one thing. Getting to the door.

"Go" he heard the whisper again.

Who in the world was talking to him? Could it be the Armor Giver? How could the Armor Giver think to even talk to him? And why did the Armor Giver let his parents be taken? He wasn't sure he wanted to hear the voice, but it gave him comfort and even courage that he was right. Though total darkness had settled in, and they could hear the shrieking, Sean was thankful for that small light that was staying just ahead of his feet. He hoped he'd see the door so they wouldn't just run right into it.

Suddenly he could see the tall mountain wall staring straight at him. He stopped and looked up at the door. It was taller than he expected. The Cedar tree carved into the door. It seemed to shine back at him. He wondered what was in the stone to make it reflect any light. He did it. He smiled quite proud of himself. He figured out the puzzle. Sean loved puzzles and loved the attention it often brought him from his Papa and Mama when he would share what he had solved. He knew what to do next. He couldn't believe he got them there safely. His father's words faded though as he loudly said

"I did it! Ravenbird, I was right! Here we are, safe! And I was right about the sky not being safe either!" Sean beamed as he spoke.

Kayleigh chimed in, "Yes, thank you Sean. But remember you heard a voice and remembered Papa's words...."

"Kayleigh can you not always sound like mom. Can't I just be a little proud that I got us here like I promised Mama and Papa I would do. Sheesh."

"Sorry, Sean. I didn't mean to hurt your feelings, I just, never mind.... thank you. Good job" Kayleigh looked behind to hide the tears that had filled her eyes.

"So, what next Sean since you figured it all out?" asked Hugh

"Alwind's song says, 'With just a knock, it will be opened."

"Since I figured it out Hugh, I'll be the one to knock! Don't even think about it, Hugh." Sean warned.

Hugh shrugged his shoulders and let his brother move to the door. It was just a knock anyways.

Chapter 7

The Wizard and His Many

Sean knocked. Nothing. Sean knocked again. Still nothing. The shrieks were growing louder. Sean kept banging on the stone till his knuckles were raw and bleeding. He fell to his knees. He failed. What did he do wrong? Kayleigh went to Sean and sat next to him. She just took his hand and put the balm she made. Sean turned to her. He mouthed sorry.

"I let you guys down. I'm so sorry. I took all the credit and forgot about the second part of the song. My heart has to be right, or it won't open. I failed. I'm sorry…I'm so…. Hugh? Hugh!?!" Panic and dread filled Sean immediately.

Sean and Kayleigh both turned and saw in horror an army approaching them. Hugh had his fists clenched and Ravenbird was talking to Hugh, but Hugh was shaking his head and had hot angry tears streaming down his face.

Sean and Kayleigh ran to Hugh. They went to grab his hand, but he shook them off and looked at them.

"You guys go! I'm going to hold them off. I'm so tired of this Wizard chasing us down. I'm going to kill that Creature of his and then go after him. You aren't going to stop me, and you need to get out of here! Go!!!" Hugh turned toward the Wizard and his many. Creature running just slightly ahead. His stupid messenger Hugh thought.

"Come and get me Creature!!!! Come and get m- "

Hugh didn't see his brother knock his legs out from under him. But he fell back hard, hard enough to knock the wind out of him.

Kayleigh pushed forward and told Sean to get Hugh and Ravenbird to the door and try once more. Sean was about to argue when he saw a familiar sight. Kayleigh threw back her hood and he could see the crown of symbols Mama had had glowing blue across the crown of her head. Without even thinking Sean scooped up Hugh. He ran knowing Kayleigh would hold her own.

Sean ran to the door all the while telling Hugh he was sorry and loved him and that he needed to be brave and go on with Ravenbird. He was their hope now. He said he believed in him and was sorry for the times he was hard on him. Hugh was a bit winded but conscious and heard every word.

"I'll stay with him Sean, but you must go back to Kayleigh quickly." Said Ravenbird.

Sean nodded in agreement and this time had just enough strength to knock on the door slightly with his forehead for his hands were full. He bent his forehead and whispered for help once more. This time to his utter surprise the door opened. He threw Hugh into the opening and Ravenbird flew in. "I love you brother!"

Sean turned to join Kayleigh and the door swiftly shut behind.

Creature was standing right in front of Kayleigh, but Kayleigh was glowing and singing the Ancient words. Sean grabbed her hand and knew this was it.

"I love you, Kayleigh!"

"I love you back brother!"

Creature sneered at them. Their words seemed to make her angrier.

"Where is the weak one! Give him to us!"

"You cannot have our brother." They both shouted.

Creature sided, "You have lost. Look, the Wizard is right here. You have lost"

Suddenly the Wizard was by Creature's side laughing. The wizard looked quite handsome. Almost like the tales the children heard of the Awe-bearers. Creatures that served the Armor Giver. Beautiful creatures that could look safe, beautiful or quite terrifying depending on the situation. They were known for their striking beauty when they came to earth. At least that's what the stories told. His voice was deep but soft. Almost hypnotic. He smiled at them with what seemed like pity in his eyes.

"Come now Creature. Let's have some pity on these poor little kids. You are mere children. And only one of you belongs to Him for now. He spat as he said that with a hint of irritation in his voice. Kayleigh did not look at him but kept saying the ancient words under her breathe."

"Sean, you and your brother are logical people. You see I have overtaken the lands. Don't be foolish like Alwind and your parents. I want you three to join me. You three are special, you see. Unique. I can see you each have talent that can benefit me and my world. The Armor Giver is not coming. Don't you see. He has given up on this place. Too many have chosen me. I can give you the power to appear and disappear and the power to have more and want more. I can give you everything here. It is mine to give. Join us? Isn't that the logical thing son?"

Sean's eyes flared as he heard the word son. Logic! How was any of this logical? He finally understood how the ancient words painted the Wizard as sneaky and a twister of words.

He grabbed his sister's hand and began joining her in the ancient words.

The creature started to cringe and scream, and the Wizard began to distort his face so that any prettiness that was there had gone. Even a darker darkness set in, and he let out a piercing gut-wrenching scream. He grew taller and an ugliness they could never describe set in.

"Foolish child! You and your sister will regret your decision! Get them!"

"With pleasure!" Creature morphed into a creature with wings yet looked almost human, except eyes covered her wings and sharp claws came from her hands and feet.

Sean and Kayleigh's crowns were both glowing bright now and they both knew they needed to be still and just speak. They don't know how, but they knew deep within that this would at least give Hugh and Ravenbird time to get to safety. Their voices grew louder as they shouted, feet firmly on the path.

"Those who belong to the Ancient One
Will not be forgotten
Will not be undone
For His light from within
Will never disappear
And when darkness come
Just call for the one
And help will always be given!"

The creature finished shifting and got ready to lead the Wizard's many against these little ones. They kept putting their hands over their ears to try and stop hearing the words.

But suddenly from behind the children another hand grabbed Sean's. Sean looked terrified as he saw it was Hugh. His best had not saved his brother. But he felt strengthened suddenly that Hugh was standing there not ready to fight but screaming the Ancient words on the top of his lungs. Maybe the Armor Giver would hear them; surely Hugh's screams could be heard above the rest.

They stood tall and steady. Kayleigh stepped a tiny bit forward to say the words again. But Hugh went in front and said "Take me! Don't hurt them! This is all my fault. Just take me but let them go!"

Hugh was going to let go but Sean and Kayleigh held on to him.

"You will not take him!" They both screamed as the creature was about to grab hold of Hugh's pants.

"Yes, we will take him! And after we will still take you!" She had some of the Wizard's many try to attack the children, but they were on the path and as they tried to reach for them the light burned them into nothingness. This angered Creature even more. Her power was stronger. She would not be killed by the path. The Wizards many were puny compared to her. She had a new plan. She whispered to some others, and she grabbed a huge stone. The others began to pick up stones to throw at Kayleigh and Sean and Hugh to knock them off the path. They would be theirs soon.

But as Creature lifted the stone to throw at Hugh, she froze and looked up, for suddenly a huge light beamed over right above the children and Creature. Ravenbird's head was glowing, and he was shifting as well. His wings widened and enlarged; his face became human like. He looked mighty and scary, yet his face was gentle. He landed behind the three and Creature and Wizard took a step back.

Ravenbird opened his mouth and light came out, as well as deep loud words that almost sounded as if they were in water. The children covered their ears but could hear clearly:

"They are NOT to be yours! Go back and get ready! The time is nearing! These are HIS!"

With that Ravenbird swept the children and pulled them quickly into the mountain and the door shut firmly to not be reopened, at least not for the Wizard. Shrieking and screams of anguish could be heard from behind but they were safe. Well, they were pretty sure they were safe.

"Ravenbird! Wait, are you a raven? What are you? Who are you? What just happened! I thought we were going to join Mama and Papa. I thought we were going to die!" Kayleigh cried out as she hugged Ravenbird.

"Forgive me children. As you can see the Wizard isn't the only one who can command what is created. I am an Awe-bearer. I was made to protect those that belong to the Armor Giver. You have become quite special to me, and the Armor Giver told me I would know when to reveal myself. He was right as usual. Kayleigh, you had chosen him long ago but Sean and Hugh, today is a day to celebrate. You have decided to trust the one who decided you would be his before time began.

Tears streamed down Sean's cheeks:

"You mean he heard my calls for help. Was that his voice I kept hearing Ravenbird?"

"Yes, Sean. He speaks in a whisper so you must be quick to listen and slow to speak as the ancient words say. And Hugh, you were slow to anger just at the right time and determined to honor your parents. Well done both of you."

The family of three looked at one another. A huge smile crossed Kayleigh's face. She hugged her brothers.

Hugh sighed. "I was ready to kill the Wizard and his creature, but I knew in the end I would be finished. And when you did all, you had to do to protect me, Sean; I knew then that Mama and Papa were right. It is better to be on the side of light and to sacrifice for good than to be on the side of the Wizard. That's when I begged Ravenbird to open the door. I was gonna do everything I could to save you and Kayleigh. I was willing to have them take me and tell you to run. Thank you Ravenbird for helping us escape. Wait, what is you real name?"

Ravenbird laughed. He suddenly became familiar and said, "Let's keep it Ravenbird shall we." The children smiled and pet Ravenbird lovingly as he had transformed to the familiar.

Now to the Ancient Tree. They took a deep breath. Whatever came, they had this peace they could never ever describe. To this day they still can't. But they somehow knew they'd be ok whatever happened. They got up and took some water and rested by the trees on the path. Finally, some shade and finally the waterbrook reappeared. It tasted better than they ever remember water tasting. Sleep overcame these three children. Ravenbird nuzzled into the midst of them.

Chapter 8

Just Speak

Sean was the first to wake. The sun seemed to be shining brighter behind the mountain. Like it used to before the darkness spread. He felt a peace settle about him as he could hear the water flowing gently over the smoothed stones of the water brook. He stretched and wiggled his legs. He saw Kayleigh asleep on his right and Hugh on his left. He smiled. Hugh always slept like a little bear curled up. Some things don't change Sean thought to himself. He felt happy at that thought.

Sean quietly got up and went over to the water brook. He felt quite thirsty. He cupped the water into his hands. The water looked so clear and felt so cool and crisp as he drank it down quickly. Ten handfuls later he heard a stirring. Kayleigh was up and looking toward the sky where Ravenbird was flying. He walked back towards her.

"Did you sleep ok Kayleigh?" asked Sean.

"I think it's the best sleep I've had since, well since that night at Alwind's house." Kayleigh smiled as she remembered that day. Life had changed so much. She sighed.

"Me too. Should we wake Hugh?"

"No, let him rest. He needs to rest after fighting so hard to make the right decision." She laughed as she said that. Sean too. They were both very proud of their younger brother.

"Ravenbird went to go get us some food."

"Come drink from the water brook. It's so tasty. I had like ten handfuls and think I'll have some more."

Kayleigh and Sean enjoyed the refreshing water. They never had water like that before.

"Is it just me Sean or does the sky seem brighter than it's been for a long time?"

"I was just thinking about that. I think the same thing. Do you think it's just behind this mountain that

The Armor Giver

the sun shines brighter? Do you think we are super close to the Ancient tree?"

"Let's ask Ravenbird when he returns. Do you know what you will say Sean? I hope the Armor Giver gives me the words to say?"

"You think He will give us the words?"

"Don't you remember Papa telling us the Ancient words say:

If you need wisdom only ask but be ready to receive the answer He has or else confusion will set in. Trust the answer He gives within."

"Man, I'm never gonna pass. I just started to do the right thing" Hugh said scratching his head and interrupting the conversation.

They all looked at each other and just burst out laughing and laughing. They had to hold their sides from laughing so hard.

"Hugh, we've come so far. I think the ancient words apply to everyone whether we started believing long ago or just yesterday." Kayleigh winked and giggled.

They hadn't noticed Ravenbird had landed behind them with food and had heard their conversation.

"It's good to hear some laughter for a change. Come eat children."

The kids smiled happily and ran to where Ravenbird was. A pile of berries and nuts were found. The kids didn't notice Ravenbird had taken multiple trips back and forth while they ate.

"Ravenbird, are we near the Ancient Tree? Will the Armor Giver tell us what to say? I feel like if I tried, I wouldn't be able to remember a thing Mama and Papa taught us once I got to that tree. You know me.... I freeze up when I take tests and mix everything up. I really will need the Armor Giver's help Ravenbird if I'm to know what to say..." Kayleigh shared her anxious thoughts.

"Now Kayleigh, whose been reminding us of all along Alwind's song and so many times the Ancient words. You have nothing to worry about! You always listened to Mama and Papa. I on the other hand was too busy making shadow animals on the wall at night when they would read. I definitely need the Armor Giver's help." Hugh said with a big sigh.

Kayleigh hugged Hugh, thankful for his sweet encouragement.

"Aww come on Hugh. You always come through in the end." Sean said matter-of-factly. Hugh's eyes grew big, and a huge smile crossed his face as he felt immense admiration for his big brother saying that. He would keep that fact to himself, but still, it was there.

"Children, I don't know what each of you will say when the time comes. But I don't think He would have sent me to watch over you and help protect you just to leave you stuck in front of the Ancient Tree, do you??" chuckled Ravenbird. The thought of those three standing in front of that tree with gray hair and wrinkles, waiting for it to open, made him giggle quite a bit, but he decided to keep that to himself as he could see the worry had not been completely wiped away.

"The Ancient Tree is close children. You will not have to worry about the Wizard for now. This is not His land. Nothing can enter without the Armor Giver's knowing and permission here. You are safe here within his boundaries."

Hearing those words brought them such relief. They looked around for the first time and realized how beautiful and peaceful and bright it was. Feeling satisfied from the food and water they laid back down on the soft grass growing by the water brook and closed their eyes to soak in the warmth of the sun.

"Ravenbird?" called Sean, remembering a question that had been on his mind since Mama and Papa left them.

"Hmm, yes?" Ravenbird replied sleepily, opening one eye. He too was enjoying the peace that seemed to hug around them.

"Ravenbird what was glowing on our heads? Mama and Papa had it too when they were fighting Creature. What does it mean?"

"What does it mean? Did your Mama and Papa not tell you yet? Well yes, I guess they would not have as they kept it hidden to not be found. When someone chooses to believe in the Armor Giver, he gives them a sign that they are his. The symbols written go from ear to ear. No one can really notice it because the hair covers it. It says:

"I am His and He is mine"

"Why does it glow?" Hugh asked scratching his head and making the face he makes when he tries to think really hard. "Does it make us powerful?" Hugh guessed. Looking very proud at his thought.

"No child. It does not make you powerful. The words glow at the moment you need Him most. Alwind needed the Giver's help the most. He needed the Armor Giver to give him courage. He needed help to let your family escape. Did you not notice their crowns glowed when darkness was heaviest and when there seemed no hope? Your parents glowed for they needed hope and help to give you time to escape. They were very brave. In fact, I was delayed in joining you children as I was busy reporting back to the Armor Giver what had happened to your family.

"Ravenbird, you saw what happened to our parents? Couldn't you have saved them like you saved us? Why didn't the Armor Giver save them? Why did he take them? We needed them…and…" Kayleigh's eyes overflowed with tears.

"My child, I just obey the Armor Giver, but He has reasons for everything and I'm sorry, but I must disagree with one thing dear. You have come so far on your own and you three have really leaned on one another. Would you have been this close had not everything happened as it has? Children what does the Armor Giver say about life here?"

Sean sighed and put his arms around Kayleigh and Hugh.

"Ravenbird has a point. I have to admit, I probably would have stayed hard on Hugh if we didn't have to stick together. I am grateful for the closeness we have. At one time I'd have given anything or anyone to have our family back. But life here is but a breath. But life with the Giver is forever. Mama and Papa and Fiona and Liam are where we are headed, they just got there first. But when it's our time, it won't end, and we will be reunited. It's hard to accept Ravenbird and yet it does give me hope." Sean smiled as he gave his brother and sister a squeeze.

Hugh shook his head in agreement. "I still wish I knew what we're supposed to say." They sat in silence for a long while.

"Well children let's go. We've rested enough. Time to head down the path."

"Ok" they said in unison. They walked down the path lazily at first. But Hugh started to feel restless and decided it was time to run.

"First one to the tree gets to talk to it Laaaasssssttt!!!!" he yelled as he started to run.

Sean and Kayleigh looked at each other and smirked. Kayleigh pushed Sean to knock him off balance and took off after Hugh. She wanted time to think. Sean quickly recovered and took off as well. They screamed and laughed and Ravenbird decided to fly versus clinging on to one of their shoulders. Ravenbird saw that they were close. He knew his orders were done. He sighed and stayed above the children soaking in their joy and laughter. He took one more look and suddenly if the children had been paying attention, they would have seen their friend was suddenly no longer with them. They were to face this task on their own.

"I see it!!!" Hugh yelled back.

"HA! I got here firs...." Hugh stared at the enormous Ancient Tree. He couldn't even see the top from where he stood. The base of the tree was very wide, and the branches started close to the base and were so thick and huge. Hugh would have climbed up right away but what he saw stopped him in his tracks. He just looked and stared at the bark covering the tree. Kayleigh and Sean arrived at the same time and found it difficult to catch their breath. They found themselves grabbing each other's hands as they looked at the beautiful, detailed carvings going around the tree in a circular pattern. They found the carvings showing the beginning of time and as they circled around the tree together, they pointed out the different stories they grew up with listening to Papa and Mama sharing every night with them. It was quite breathtaking. The intricate details and the beauty of this tree just left them in silence for quite some time.

"Ravenbird.... I've never seen a tree as beautiful as this one.... Ravenbird.... Ravenbird?" Kayleigh said as she looked around to find their friend.

"Where is he?"

"Maybe he went to find us food?" shrugged Hugh

"I wonder if.... hmmm.... never mind." Sean said quietly. He wondered if they'd see their friend again.

The Amor Giver

He wasn't so sure. He knew they'd need to face this task without any help. He suddenly felt very unsure of himself and a bit stressed but didn't want to worry Hugh and Kayleigh, so he looked like he was super busy being focused on the pictures carved into the tree. In reality he was talking to himself. Trying to recall the words Papa and Mama would tell them before bed. But for the life of him, he was mixing stories and words together. "Ugh what am I going to tell the Armor Giver?" he asked himself. "What do you want me to say?"

"Sean, when do you think it will be time to say something? I'm super nervous and a little scared if I'm to be honest." shared Kayleigh.

"I'm not sure sis. But I'm nervous too. Would you mind singing Alwind's song to us? Maybe it will help us remember more of Mama and Papa's words."

"Yeah KK, please sing?" asked Hugh.

KK closed her eyes and tried to picture Mama and Papa sitting by the fireplace where they'd gather every night. Kayleigh's beautiful voice rose:

Above the clouds

Above our lands

Above the dark and evil hands

Hear my child in this song

The secret hope that can be found

Follow down

The narrow path

Run my child

Do not look back

The shield of light
It will protect you
Run my child
Do not look back
The shield of light
It will protect you
Run my child
Run to the mountain
To the Doors of Cedars

Seek the truth
And you will find
Which door to take
Which is right
With just a knock
It will be opened
With good intentions
Or you'll be forbidden

Look for the ancient words
Inscribed on the Ancient tree
From birth you will have
known them
Read them right for
They must be spoken
If you are worthy
The gift will be given
Beware of yourself
use only when right
Or it will be taken

The Amor Giver

For it holds the secret light
That will send away
The Wizard and his many
And reveal what is hidden
Hush my child
You must Listen
Hush my child
You must Listen
Follow the whisper
Watch out for the Wizard
Follow the whisper
And help will come
from the Armor Giver
Yes, help will come
From the Armor Giver..........

Just as Kayleigh finished singing the Ancient tree began to glow. A bright blue light emerged from the carving around the tree. The children stood in awe. Hugh was curious how the light was coming forth through the tree, so he went toward it. Suddenly he could see words forming in through the stories carved.

"What...hey do you see this? Do you see the word...." He began reading them aloud, "Action is the proof of what you believe. Hugh, do you believe?" Hugh's eyes grew big, and he wanted to run but something was pulling him through. He thought back through his life. Tears filled his eyes. "I believe!", he shouted back." I believe, but I don't always do what I should. I'm sorry but I know now that you can help me! Help me Armor Giver...."

Suddenly Sean and Kayleigh could no longer see Hugh. He was gone. They ran together toward the light still coming from the tree.

"I can see the words, Kayleigh. Do you?" asked Sean.

Kayleigh shook her head. I just see the beautiful light. What words do you see Sean?"

Sean looked up and said, "If you knew everything, all of the secrets of the world and held all the answers but did not love others – nothing you would be! Sean, you hold great knowledge, do you love?" Sean's eyes grew big, and tears dripped down his cheeks. He lowered his head meekly and whispered "Lord, I cannot love without your help. I don't do it very well. I often get busy learning everything and I forget to have it hit my heart. I need your help. Please help...."

"Sean don't leave me! Armor Giver where are my brothers? Please don't leave me alone?" Kayleigh cried as she circled around the tree.

As she looked up, she saw the light begin to move and words begin to form. She stepped closer. What would it say to her. She closed her eyes and took a deep breath. "Don't be afraid Kayleigh. You are never alone."

She opened her eyes and read the words, "Do not worry about anything but tell the Armor Giver everything and thank Him, remember what he's already done and peace that no one can understand will fill you up and guard you."

"Armor Giver, I try to remember to talk to you. I'm sorry I get so busy trying to take care of everything that I forget to thank you and tell you what I'm feeling. Help me do this more. I cannot be on my own. I worry for my family and worry about the dangers. Help me trust you, help me to…" and then suddenly, no one was standing by the Ancient Tree, and no one saw the blue light fade away until only the beauty of the scenery was left.

Chapter 9

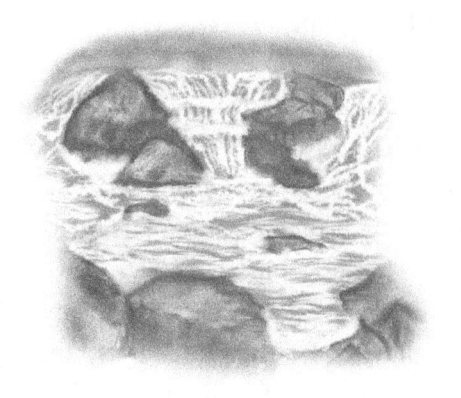

The Secret

As soon as they had found their footing, they grabbed for each other's hands.

Bright light surrounded Hugh, Sean, and Kayleigh and yet they were able to keep their eyes open. They stood trying to focus and see past the light that engulfed them. It was so quiet, so peaceful. The panic that would have once overcome them was no longer there. Instead, they saw enough ahead of them to walk forward. Step by step was all they could see. Suddenly they saw a figure coming toward them. They could only tell because the light that poured out from the figure was blue. The children kept taking steps forward. The blue light seemed to show another figure coming with the other. Their eyes continued to look ahead. Suddenly two smaller lights pushed past the other two figures and seemed to be running.

"Is that laughter?" the three wondered. The laughter sounded so familiar. So sweet and wild. Their eyes widened and they looked at each other. Could it be? Could it really be possible?

Hugh started laughing and made the other two run with him. The little blue lights jumped up onto the three and Kayleigh cried so happily, "Liam and Fiona?!? Is that really you?" They just kept jumping up and down and laughing and crying and in the midst of the chaos you could hear Fiona sing out, "My brothers and sister!! I am so happy! I am so happy!" While the reunited 5 were having such a happy reunion, they didn't notice the other two lights that had finally caught up to the little ones.

"Well, I think we're long overdue for a wrestle, don't you?"

"Papa!!!" the boys screamed. They felt their Papa's strong arms around them, and they just folded into little clumps, crying and hugging and just clinging tightly to their Papa.

"Kayleigh girl, I'm so proud of you my brave girl." Mama said as she picked her up and held her tight. Kayleigh was so happy and just couldn't believe her Mama was holding her.

"Oh Mama! Mama, how? I saw what happened. How did you survive? Are you real Mama? Are you really here? Kayleigh asked in disbelief. She didn't want to pinch herself in case this was a dream.

Mama smiled and just hugged her daughter tightly. "I am here sweet girl. This is very real. Answers will come soon Kayleigh girl. But for now, let me look at you. You made it. My precious three you all made it." Everyone gathered together and just held on tight.

"Well, this is a happy sight!"

"Ravenbird!!!" the kids called out.

"Ravenbird, you knew our parents and Fiona and Liam were alive and didn't tell us." Hugh said, half frowning.

"Now Hugh, remember, my job is to obey the words given. I could not share this good news with you. But I am so happy you know now. I was summoned to protect you three and to keep you safe. Just as the light flashed, I was given orders to grab your Mama and Papa and sister and brother. I was delayed in getting to you three, but I think it was good I was delayed, don't you?" asked Ravenbird as he gave a little nod to Hugh's family. Hugh nodded in agreement and went back to squeezing his Mama. He had missed her so. (But that was a fact he'd keep to himself). Sean went over and leaned his head on his Mama. He had missed her too.

He looked around and just wanted this memory to sear into his brain to be kept forever. All the pain seemed to melt. All the built-up anger and frustration seeped away as thankfulness overwhelmed him.

"Well Family of Seven, it's now time for the 3 to meet the Armor Giver. Come with me." Ravenbird said as he went upward.

"But how in the world are we to .... oh!!!" Hugh exclaimed as he found himself effortlessly following Ravenbird's direction. "Hey Sean, I guess you don't have to worry about gravity up here?" They all giggled and felt a rush of excitement as they seemed to glide across the sky.

The bright light continued to surround them and then stairs that seemed golden appeared and they came to a huge wall. The walls were enormous. Colors of every gemstone you could think of went on and on in a beautiful pattern. What looked like the biggest pearls the kids had ever seen were in the middle of the wall like doors. Ravenbird stopped at the doors and said, "He is theirs and they are his!" Suddenly the pearl doors slid apart into the wall, and they walked through. Here they stepped onto solid ground which shone with golden hues and looked almost transparent gold. While Sean enjoyed floating, he felt a little relieved to be walking on something solid.

The children clung tightly to their parents' hands. Liam and Fiona skipped ahead. Liam ran as always looking behind and kept bumping into Fiona, but they just laughed. The kids looked around them as they walked quickly to keep up with Liam and Fiona. They couldn't believe what they saw. It looked like their world, but the colors were stunning. The streets shone like gold and the houses were colorful like gemstones and the nature that surrounded each home was just so luminescent. And yet a bright light still shone all around. But it seemed to compliment everything. The flowers, the trees, the pathways, the stones were so vibrant and alive. There were flowers Kayleigh had never seen before. Winding through the streets was a beautiful flowing brook.

Beyond them was what looked like the biggest castle they'd ever seen but they stopped before the pathway to it.

Sean saw what looked like a man sitting in front of the pathway. His eyes looked kind. Liam and Fiona jumped into his lap and whispered in his ear quite loudly "They made it! They're here! Just like you said." He whispered something back into their ears and they quickly hugged him and went back to Mama and Papa. The three felt suddenly like they knew this person.

"Hello Sean, Kayleigh and Hugh. Well done children." the man said gently. His smile was so kind, and his eyes seemed to look straight into their hearts and minds.

"Are you he? Are you the Armor Giver?" Kayleigh asked. She always pictured him as someone quite serious looking, tall and strong, and maybe even wearing some type of warrior clothing. This man looked quite ordinary, and nothing really stood out except his smile. His smile brought her instant calm and peace.

"I am he." He said, "You three have done so so well. I'm so sorry you had to go through so much to get here children, and without your Mama and Papa and brother and sister, but you have made me so happy and proud. You have beaten the very fears and struggles that often kept you from seeing me. Kayleigh girl well done leading your brothers to me.

"How did I do that?" she asked.

"By being there. By reminding them of my words, by believing from the beginning and never giving up. And Sean, you too kept my words close to you, but to see you finally trust in them and desire to actually believe; You chose to love and not just lean on logic. Well done son. "

Sean beamed and soaked in what the Armor Giver was saying. He did feel so different. The love he felt for his family had deepened so much. Love in general meant so much more to him now.

"And Hugh. Come here, Hugh."

Hugh immediately went up to him and jumped into his arms giving him a big hug.

"Hugh, you conquered many struggles, you worked so hard, didn't you?"

Hugh nodded, allowing some tears to drop down his cheeks but then he smiled and said, "But I did it! It was so hard, but I felt so happy after choosing to do the right thing. But you helped me, didn't you?"

"I always help those who ask for it. But the choice is always theirs, always yours, you understand?"

"The Wizard and Creature have tricked so many down there. It really seems like he is winning.... but he isn't right? Hugh asked.

The Armor Giver just smiled and stood up. He looked at the Family of Seven.

"Oh Ravenbird, you did so well my friend. Thank you for being so faithful to the task."

"Wait, if Mama and Papa and Fiona and Liam are here, does that mean Alwind didn't die too?" Sean asked looking around to see if he could see Alwind.

Ravenbird bowed low and looked up and saw it was time for the secret to be told. He gave a quick bow to the Armor Giver and flew off.

"Do we get to come with you to your castle now that they made it here?" Fiona interrupted.

The Armor Giver laughed and said "Oh Fiona, you've been so patient, haven't you? The castle is for later but come with me. I want to show you and your family something. Let's go walk along the water brook.

They walked in silence, but no one was bored. The peacefulness around them felt so refreshing and energizing. They felt protected and safe here. Before they knew it, they looked out and saw that the water brook had expanded into a beautiful lake. In front of it was an ever-expanding green meadow. The grass felt so soft as they walked on it. The Armor Giver smiled and pointed to an area that had a huge soft blanket on the ground and plates of food. The kids ran to it and sat down taking in all the dishes. Mama and Papa sat down beside them.

"Wow – look at all these dishes. It's all our favorite dishes Mama! Did you make these?" asked Hugh.

"No son," laughed Mama. "Every day these dishes arrive. Isn't it amazing. And every day the Armor Giver sat with us as we waited for you to come." She squeezed Hugh's hand.

Everyone ate until they were satisfied and while the Armor Giver played a little game of tag with Liam and Fiona, the other three cuddled closely to their Mama and Papa, soaking in every second with their parents.

After a while, Liam and Fiona crawled in their Mama's lap and fell asleep. The Armor Giver sat down and said, "Well that was fun. Oh, that mankind would stay as children, innocent and full of life." He sighed as he said that. "Well Family of Seven.... I must tell you the secret that I have been waiting to tell you. I am happy to have you stay with me till the end but there is a special job I have that I would like to entrust to you. It will not be easy, but I believe many more can be saved from the Wizard and his many through your family. There are others like you, but they have been captured. The Wizard has taken the ones he sees most threatening and has sealed them in his dungeons. He hasn't killed them because he wants to break their spirit. To fill them with darkness, to torture them by showing them he is winning. He feeds them just enough to keep them alive and often shows them when another has chosen the shadows. It will take much courage, but these others, if freed, will be able to work with you to save many more who dwell in the shadows. One of these prisoners is someone you know very well…Alwind.

Everyone gasped a little. Alwind wasn't dead. He was captured. "But what are they doing to him?"

"Alwind is being very brave children. But he's very tired. I have sent a watcher to watch over him and to give him strength, but the time is coming for the final battle and these faithful few are needed. The Wizard doesn't know the Secret. But the Secret is this: Those who belong to me, always belong to me and will rise together. Where my people are, I am there too. And when they work together – they cannot be easily broken. The battle is already won. It is now time to finish the Wizard and his many and start again. But I would like your family to join in my battle. What do you say?" asked the Armor Giver, smiling gently.

"Are you kidding me?!? Be part of your army and go save Alwind? YES!! YES!! YES!!!…oops I mean what do you think Mama and Papa?" Hugh sheepishly slowed down to ask.

Papa laughed. "That's my son. Well, I already thought I died once and yet here we are all together. I know there will be very dangerous moments, but I think we've been through enough to know that we aren't alone. If you give us this task, then with your help, it will be done."

The Armor Giver smiled and said, "Very True. You are definitely right. And you will not be alone as Ravenbird will be by your side…."

"What about the Armor?" asked Sean excitedly.

"You have it." Smiled the Armor Giver.

"Where?"

"Do you remember what Ravenbird said about when you choose to believe what sign is there to show you belong to me?"

"Oh wait, the crown is our armor?" asked Kayleigh.

"Yes, do you know how?"

The children shook their heads.

"Well, here is the secret: when your parents needed me most, they called out the Ancient Words and held hands and the light that came from their crowns pushed back the darkness. I am the Armor. Do you see? You are never alone. You must remember this. The Wizard doesn't understand this. He wants you to believe you are alone, he wants to separate and destroy. You will still need to be careful when you go back. It will be even darker where I am sending you. But I believe you 7 can fight together to free the few faithful and then work with them to help the shadow dwellers come to the light. I know I'm asking a lot. Kayleigh, what do you think."

Kayleigh thought a long while and then smiled. "I think that I believe in you, when you say we won't be alone, I already thought I lost my Mama and Papa and my hope was that I would see them again. No matter what happens, I know for sure now that what the

Wizard brings is just fake arrows to try and scare me. The worst that could happen is that my family comes back here and at different times but for sure we will be back. That gives me peace. I think we really can do this for you. I think we can work together, but I worry for Liam and Fiona. They are so young.

The Armor Giver picked up Fiona and Liam. "These little ones will surprise you, Kayleigh. These two pushed past your Mama and Papa singing the ancient words just before Ravenbird came to get them. They were very brave."

Kayleigh said, "Well then, I'm just happy we all get to do this task together. When do we begin?"

"Well, first you all deserve a rest. You will rest here in the field. Nothing will bother you. Sleep and when it's time we will wake you and go over the task."

Everyone suddenly felt very tired. They all happily laid down on the huge soft blanket and even though the light never faded, they slept so easily. And each member of the Family of Seven could be seen sleeping with a smile on their face. This place felt so comfortable. And being with the Armor Giver felt like being reunited with someone who you always knew and loved. They didn't want to leave but each were determined to free Alwind. He was in jail because he protected them. With each other together again, they knew they'd be able to face the Wizard and his many. Hugh especially couldn't wait to see Creature again; he'd be ready to fight this time with his new crown. The Family of Seven had no worries for that day. The

Armor Giver looked on as they rested. He'd let them wake up on their own and then he'd prepare them for the task that lay ahead.

Chapter 10

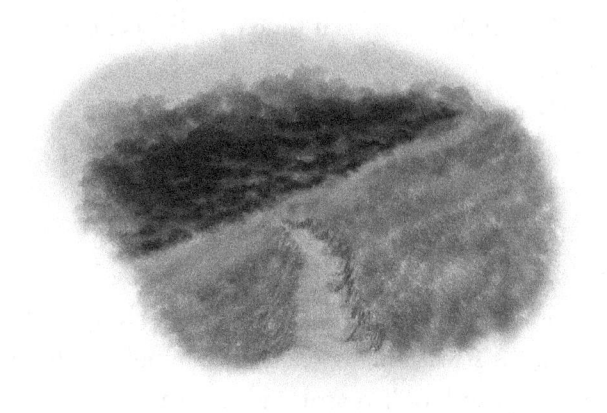

The Task

Mama opened her eyes. She looked around and smiled. Surrounded by her babies, she soaked in the peacefulness of it all. What a treasure to be here. She sighed and felt a sudden desire to just stay there forever but her mind shifted to Alwind. Dear Alwind. They owed so much to him. Liam yawned and opened his eyes and saw his Mama was up. So, he climbed over

Sean and Kayleigh and plopped onto his Mama. Mama smiled and squeezed her little one. He looked at her and then looked at his stomach and Mama knew exactly what he was about to say.

"Mama..."

"Yes Liam?"

"Is it time to eat?"

"Not just yet but let's go for a walk."

"Ok, in this many is it time to eat?" as he held up 5 fingers.

Mama laughed and took him by the hand to go for a walk while the others slept.

Sean woke up next, as he always woke up early. He opened his eyes and saw Mama was gone and panicked but then turned to his left and saw Papa's big arm by his shoulder and Papa deep in sleep. He sighed and smiled. "It's real, this is real." He thought to himself. He got up and looked around the meadow. He picked a few blades of grass and enjoyed examining their texture and how they felt. Sean couldn't believe they were all together and safe. He closed his eyes and quietly thanked the Armor Giver for bringing his family back together. While he eyes were still closed, he suddenly felt someone grabbing him and lifting him off the ground but just as quickly found himself and the other person tumbling onto the grassy meadow.

Thump...." oomph!" a booming voice was echoing in Sean's ear. He immediately started laughing.

"Well, I don't remember you being big enough to knock the air out of me Sean boy." said Papa as he rolled Sean off of him and laughed as he clutched his stomach. They both laughed and laughed as they tried to get back up, but the laughter kept making them double over.

Hugh and Kayleigh and Fiona woke up to the laughter and smiled looking at each other. The girls nodded in agreement with Hugh and when Hugh shouted "NOW!!!!", the three of them jumped on Papa tackling him back toward the ground. Liam came running out of nowhere and everyone sort of braced themselves as he jumped headfirst into the pile. Papa caught him just before his head hit Fiona's.

Laughter filled the place of rest. The Armor Giver watched as this Family of Seven filled their hearts with joy. He loved it when his people loved well. To him, this was good. He let them rest for a moment longer and then made his way to them. Fiona saw him first. She ran to him and gave him a hug and took his hand to walk with him.

"Armor Giver?" she asked

"Yes, Fiona? "

"Once we save Alwind, can we come back?" her eyes looked full of concern.

"Yes Fiona. You may always come back and soon you may always stay."

"Yay!!" Fiona said. And as they walked to the rest she sang:

"Once we save Alwind, we can come back! And in fact, we can always come back!

Yes, he said we can always come back and soon he said we will always stay! "

The family stood up smiling, ready to hear what the Armor Giver had to say. Ravenbird flew down and rested on Hugh's shoulder. Hugh smiled and gave Ravenbird a little pet. He then hopped over to Kayleigh and gave her a little peck.

"Hello Armor Giver!" the family happily greeted him.

"Hello, my Family of Seven, did you rest well?"

"I feel like I rested for a month!" Hugh said.

"Good. We will have some breakfast together but first I want to go over the task that you will have while you are away. Please sit down."

The Task:

Follow the narrow path
Until it turns into the widened road
Journey into the shadowlands
To the Wizards Lair you must go

Follow into the Darkened Forest
It will take you to the shadowlands
Beware of the Wizard and his many
For they will try to take your hand

There will be those that seem
To be a follower of light
But wolves you see they really be
You must be ready to give flight at night
When it happens, you'll see

There is a helper along the way
She is the key to the lair
Her gift will be seen in what she will say
She is good and not of the many

You will know it is her
By the way she answers
But the questions must
Be one of mine
So, remember my words
And you'll know what to say
She will answer, you'll know she is mine

With her go to the shadowlands
Creature will be waiting
Be careful to stay true to me
For Creature, it is cunning

Creature will take you to the Lair
Thinking that all is in their hands
Go with the beast to their darkened land
And clearly you will see my plan

The Wizard is strong there
It is his domain
But ask for my help
It will not be in vain

> Now if one of you is lost or gone
> Remember it's not forever
> But if you remember the Armor
> You're given
> Then together with Alwind you will be risen

"This is the Task. I will help you remember these words. Fiona, I bet you can help your family by putting this into a song. We will work together on this later. You will stay here a few days longer so I can prepare you"

Fiona smiled wide and nodded, squeezing the Armor Giver's hand.

"The task is dangerous. Alwind isn't the only one I want you to save. Along the way there is a girl, her family was captured by Creature and is in prison with Alwind. They were helping me reach the people of the East just as your family and Alwind were reaching the people of the West. The daughter is hiding and is very alone. But she has not given up. She is in the Darkened Forest. She needs your help. She is the key to getting you to the Wizards lair. Nothing is what it seems in the shadowlands. There are also those that claim to be mine.... but they belong to the Wizard, disguising themselves as lightkeepers but really, they are wolves of darkness. The wizard knows you are coming, but he cannot harm you. He and I have spoken and as long as you get through you will be allowed through, for our final battle has not yet come. But he can try to make you fail, Family of Seven. There is no lighted path for you are headed into the widened pathways. But you will see a light leading you step by step. No one around you can see it, but Creature can smell the light. Be alert. Remember my words. Remember who you know me to be."

"There will be times your armor will be needed, children. Your crowns glowed however your armor did not appear as you had not met with me yet. You see once you ask for help and say the Ancient Words, there I will be covering you with the Armor that is needed for that moment. Depending on the situation a piece or pieces of armor will cover you. Sean, I believe you saw Alwind shine from a far and wondered what was reflecting around him?" asked the Armor Giver.

Sean nodded, amazed that the Armor Giver had seen that.

The Armor Giver continued, "Alwind had my full covering to fight off the Wizard and his many and give you time to escape. He used my sword to push back the enemy and the full armor to protect him from what Creature and the Wizard's many tried to throw at him. Once you escaped however, Alwind grew tired and accidentally stepped off the path which allowed Creature to grab him. However, there is a reason I allowed this. If you are successful, not only Alwind will be saved. This is why he stepped off the path. Your parents also had my shield around them till Ravenbird could grab them. Do you know the pieces of armor Mama and Papa? Asked the Armor Giver, turning to them.

They nodded and smiled. Papa excitedly said,

"You see children the Armor Giver is always ready to help. Depending on what is needed when the crown glows, you will be given one or two or all of the these:

Help is given
When He is called
Say His words
The Dark will Fall

Stand your ground
He will give to you
What you need
To see you through

The belt of truth
Exposes lies
His body Armor
Keeps you right

The shoes of peace
Puts all at ease
The shield of faith
Helps you escape

The helmet that saves
Will keep you from undoing
The sword of his word
Will bring Wizard to ruin

The Family of Seven sat in silence, deep silence for a long while. Suddenly a little voice piped in:

"Can we have breakfast now? Has it been this many yet?" asked Liam holding up his little five fingers for everyone to see.

Everyone laughed and hugged Liam. The Armor Giver laughed the loudest and picked up Liam and put him on his shoulders.

"Come Family of Seven, let's go eat!"

Off they walked to the pasture. Together they sat and ate all their favorites again and laughter could be heard and Fiona's little voice already humming a melody she would teach her family to remember the Task. She danced around as she hummed and hummed. Sean and Kayleigh and Hugh linked arms and Sean reached to squeeze Papa's hand and Hugh squeezed Mama's and Kayleigh scooped Liam into her lap. They planned to treasure every minute left here in the pasture and Liam intended on enjoying every bite.

The End...well for now.

Epilogue

Throwing moldy flat bread at his feet, Creature snickered.

"Eat up Alwind. You have to eat eventually. You are skin and bones old man."

"I don't need your bread Creature. Go back to your Wizard. You make such a good puppet." snickered Alwind.

Creature growled and grabbed Alwind roughly, for he had shifted into a shape that would let him grab him. He mirrored Alwind's face and said

"You are weak, you are pathetic. Even you tell yourself this. Hahahaha!!!" it laughed throwing Alwind across the floor roughly and then stepping on the bread as it walked out of the cell. As it walked away laughing, it shifted back into its horrible being.

Alwind grimaced and pulled himself up. He closed his eyes and began as he always did.

"Armor Giver, you gave me another day. Thank you for it might not come again tomorrow. Your word is the bread I need. Please give me a word from you because I am tired. I am old. I am finding it harder to be happy that I made it to another day. Help me...." Doors opened.

Alwind opened his eyes and tried to focus to see what was going on or hear what the voices were saying. Suddenly the door to his room opened and he saw shadows being thrown toward him. He winced as their bodies crashed down hard and the door slammed behind them.

"Owww"

"Ugh"

"Ouch!"

"Oma! Apa!!" little scared voices cried out.

Alwind recognized those little voices. "Yehoon? Yewan? Is that you?"

"Alwind!!!" they ran over to the old man and jumped on him. He suddenly felt big arms grip him and pull him up and a laugh that brought him so much joy.

"Oh Alwind!! We were so worried when we didn't hear from you for many months. We came looking for you and look we found you!!! I wish we found you somewhere nicer though, maybe at your home with rice and kimchi." Everyone's stomach made music at Hoony's sentence. They all laughed.

"Hoony and Eun!!!" Alwind exclaimed. Oh, his favorite family of 5. He closed his eyes and thanked the Armor Giver for giving him what he needed to get through another day at the Wizard's shadow lair. But their group hug felt incomplete. Where was Yeyang?

Alwind looked at Eun and before he could ask, she burst into tears. "We were taken from her. We went looking for you Alwind when you hadn't come for many months. We got to your home, and it was empty. We thought we would be safe but didn't notice that your place had been visited already by the Wizard. He left his shadow men behind. We went to sleep, and you know Yeyang. She chose to sleep in the tree near your home Alwind. You know how she loves to be in that tree looking up to the sky. The kids woke up early, so we took them for a walk. Just as we were going to return, we walked into Creature; the shadow men had told them we were at Alwind's. They took us and Yeyang was left behind. We don't know if they took her or if she escaped. I don't know what to do Alwind. I miss her so much…," cried Eun. Everyone sat down and tears just fell.

Alwind closed his eyes. This was too much. He let out a deep sigh and took their hands. He looked each of them in the eyes and suddenly they knew what they needed to do.

They huddled together and a song arose. It rose high above the lair of the wicked Wizard. The shadow dwellers held their ears and Wizard and Creature screeched in pain. The words were bringing physical pain to their bodies.

"O Armor Giver
Where your Word is
You are there

O Armor Giver
Though there's darkness
In the air

I will choose to cheer
For He is coming
he's coming
To drive out all the
darkness

Yes, he's coming to take away the Wizard and his darkness"

As the song rose, many around them writhed on the floor and covered their ears. In the midst of the writhing no one noticed the little black bird flying swiftly down the lair and into the prison. No one noticed him descend into the little huddled group of singers. And no one saw the little smile that cracked across Alwind's face as he looked at the little black bird and gave it a little wink. They just heard Alwind's voice grow annoyingly louder....

To be continued....

About Kharis Publishing:

Kharis Publishing, an imprint of Kharis Media LLC, is a leading Christian and inspirational book publisher based in Aurora, Chicago metropolitan area, Illinois. Kharis' dual mission is to give voice to under-represented writers (including women and first-time authors) and equip orphans in developing countries with literacy tools. That is why, for each book sold, the publisher channels some of the proceeds into providing books and computers for orphanages in developing countries so that these kids may learn to read, dream, and grow. For a limited time, Kharis Publishing is accepting unsolicited queries for nonfiction (Christian, self-help, memoirs, business, health and wellness) from qualified leaders, professionals, pastors, and ministers. Learn more at: https://kharispublishing.com/

www.ingramcontent.com/pod-product-compliance
Lightning Source LLC
LaVergne TN
LVHW020816140125
801165LV00006B/173